COWBOY'S BEST SHOT

Melissa,
Always give it your
best shot 😊

Lexi Post

Melissa,

Always give it your
best shot 😊

[signature]

COWBOY'S
BEST SHOT

LEXI POST

Cowboy's Best Shot

Cowboy Hunter McKade is former military police who survived two tours overseas. When he came home, his wife and his life as he knew it, disappeared in an instant. Now a security guard at Poker Flat Nudist Resort, he exists in his dark place, requiring little social interaction – until the night he breaks the barrier that separates him from *her*.

As a former prostitute from a high-end bordello, Adriana Perez loves sex – any kind, anywhere – and her rules are few. Her new bartending job at Poker Flat gives her lots of hospitality opportunities, so why is someone trying to get her fired? Baffled, she gratefully accepts Hunter's help and protection, and is more than willing to show him her appreciation. But the man has far too much control.

Pushing Hunter beyond his boundaries becomes Adriana's satisfying distraction. But the evidence against her mounts, and she ignores her gut to take matters into her own hands. Unfortunately, her best shot at fixing this may not be enough to save her job…or her heart.

Keep up with Lexi Post Updates by signing up for her monthly newsletter here www.lexipostbooks.com.

Acknowledgments

For Robert A. Fabich, Sr., former Air Force Security Police and present day hero of my heart. And for my sister Paige Wood, who's always willing to listen whenever I need an ear.

A special thank you to Army Captain Robert A. Fabich, Jr., for serving our country and for sharing his experience and knowledge with me.

I don't know what I'd do without my wonderful critique partner, Marie Patrick, who is the only known antidote for my severe allergy to question marks. Thank you!

Lastly, thank you to Grace Bradley, my editor, who teaches me something new with every book.

AUTHOR'S NOTE

Cowboy's Best Shot was inspired by a story and a meditation. The short story is Bret Harte's *The Outcasts of Poker Flat*, first published in 1869. In Harte's story, four members of Poker Flat society—a gambler, a prostitute, a madam, and a drunk—are banned from the western settlement when a sudden urge to be virtuous overtakes the citizens. On their way to the next settlement, the outcasts stop to rest at the base of some high mountains. An innocent couple comes down from the mountains and rests with them. This cast of characters explores the relationship between the innocent and the tainted in Harte's story.

But what happens when the innocent becomes tainted? Can he ever go back? Does he want to? And is love still a possibility, or is it just a shot in the dark?

The meditation is by 17th Century poet John Donne and is titled *Meditation XVII* from *Devotions Upon Emergent Occasions*. The two phrases most quoted from this work are "No man is an island" and "For whom the bell tolls; it tolls for thee." It focuses on the idea that all men and women are connected to each other because they are part of the human race.

Can an individual live among others and remain unconnected,

an island, if she wanted to? If she could, what would be the benefits and shortfalls of such a life?

Chapter One

Adriana Perez pulled against the ropes that bound her wrists to the foot of the bed as lube ran down her crease. Being tied wasn't her favorite sex play, but a little was okay on occasion. She was just too far from being a submissive to really enjoy it.

The threesome staying at Poker Flat Nudist Resort was proving to be one of the better hookups she'd had in a long while. They at least had experience and appeared to be taking her challenge to them seriously—make her come.

She stood bent over, her wrists tied to the short footboard of the bed. The inside of the casita was lit by three lamps, leaving them all on display in the sliding glass door to her right. Not that it mattered, it was a nudist resort, and most of the guests were in their own casitas probably having their own fun. Besides, it was well after 1:00 a.m.—as that's when she'd closed the bar for the night.

The woman sitting on the floor beneath her had picked out two toys to use. The man behind her spread her ass as the cool liquid ran across her anal star and followed her flesh until it dripped to the floor.

The other man knelt on the bed, nipple clamps in his hands. Anticipation raced through her. She might actually orgasm this time without—

The cold metal of one clamp latched on to her right nipple. It was nothing new, but it did build some anticipation. He wrapped the chain over her neck and clamped the other metal clip to her left nipple. Her stomach tightened. This could prove enjoyable. As she moved her neck, the clamps pulled. Nice.

When he reached around her again, she held her breath, hoping he would tighten the clamps. He didn't disappoint. Her core clenched as the metal pinched her flesh. He sat back on the bed and nodded to the man behind her.

Finally, it would begin. She'd been a prostitute in her past life at a very exclusive bordello in Nevada. She'd done it not just for the money, but because she enjoyed sex. All kinds of sex. When she moved to Arizona to become Poker Flat's bartender, she found she missed the sex. Luckily, the resort opened and she'd been able to enjoy a few good lays.

The problem was that most of the people who stayed at a nudist resort were not into alternative lifestyles. They simply liked not wearing clothes. But occasionally swingers booked a couple casitas and they were always open to another woman.

The pressure of a hard cock against her anal hole had her grasping the footboard. The woman beneath her, Tina was her name, took that moment to press a vibrating dildo against her clit. "Ah, now that's what I'm talking about."

Tina didn't answer, probably didn't do anything her two

Dominants didn't want her to do. When the vibration pulled away, Adriana glanced at her to see she'd turned on a vibrating bullet. There was more to sex than vibration, but she wasn't going to complain.

The cock behind her started to rub up and down her crease. The teasing motion had her pushing back. The smack of a hand on her ass stung. "Ow. What the hell? Don't spank me again or I'm out of here."

The man behind her chuckled. "That might be a little hard, tied to the bed."

She looked over her shoulder. What was his name? Tom? John? Something generic. "Don't push it."

"Whatever."

The man in front of her tsked and lifted her chin to look at him as he knelt before her. "Not smart to confront the most dominant."

"I told you, I'm not a submissive, nor do I want to be. You all agreed. Besides…" She paused as the woman slid the vibrating bullet inside her. Her sheath clenched it, happy to have the stimulation she craved. "You have this pretty thing under me. You don't need me."

The man behind her grunted. "True. But I am going to enjoy fucking your ass hole."

Despite his crudity, her core tensed. She used to serve a very classy clientele and they all enjoyed their own special kink. She'd just think of this as slumming.

"And I want to fuck that gorgeous mouth of yours." The man on the bed stroked her lips with his cock. "Would you like that?"

She grinned. This man she could handle just fine. She shot her tongue out and licked at the cock head in front of her. It wasn't long. She could easily take it in, but it was wide. She'd always been known for her big mouth. She smirked before nipping at the tip.

She opened her lips and sucked the cock halfway inside. The vibrating dildo made contact with her clit again, sending pleasure waves up to meet those being produced by the bullet, but that she could do on her own. It was the two men who were her hope for something more.

The rubbing along her ass crack slowed and she felt cool lube glide all around the cock head between her cheeks. She opened her mouth, allowing the cock in front of her to enter all the way. Being fucked from both ends had its own rewards.

Then the pressure built at her anal hole. She relaxed her muscles there as the woman pulled the dildo away from her clit and pushed it into her sheath until it met the bullet.

The man behind her grunted as he pushed in. "Fuck that's good."

The double vibration in her tight ass was making him happy. She turned her head to the side, keeping the cock in her mouth, and the nipple clamps pulled. That was better.

The woman beneath her must have realized the double vibration in her sheath wasn't enough and pulled it out to lay the dildo against her clit. Now, with the cock gliding in and out of her anal hole and the one in her mouth mimicking the motion, her tension finally built.

The vibrator against her clit started to circle and a tongue licked across her clamped right nipple. Yes, this was what she wanted. The orgasmic release that was like her own drug. The men in her ass and mouth started to lose control as they rocked into her.

The tiny bites on her compressed nipple sent excitement colliding with the waves of tension building inside her vibrating sheath.

She was revved and ready but the sensations plateaued. Disappointment crept over her. She turned her head to the other side, just needing more, more feeling, pulling on the chain attached to her nipples. She needed someone watching.

Then in the darkness outside, a pair of black cowboy boots stepped into the light thrown from the sliders onto the patio.

Him.

Adriana caught her breath as every pleasurable sensation suddenly collided. Her orgasm hit hard, sending adrenaline racing along every artery, providing the satisfaction she craved.

She closed her eyes and the man on the bed came inside her mouth just as the one behind her yelled. The ecstasy left quickly, the moment gone as fast as it had come. It was as if she'd built up a tolerance to orgasms. Maybe she needed to lay off the toys for a while, dry out.

Yeah, who was she kidding?

She spit out the cock in her mouth and looked back to the patio. He was gone. She let her head drop, unconcerned that she was still tied and a bullet continued to buzz in her pussy.

The man behind her slowly pulled out. Instinct had her looking over her shoulder. "Don't even think about it."

He scowled, his hand raised to smack her ass. "I think you need to be taught a lesson."

"I don't need any lessons from you."

His tense face relaxed and he smirked. "Who said anything about me? Tina?"

The woman beneath her looked out at her Dom. "Yes, Sir."

"I want you to suck on this woman's clit while I wash up. If we make her come a second time, both Gary and I will fuck you at the same time. If she doesn't come, then neither will you…all night."

The woman simply nodded.

Adriana looked at him and raised her eyebrow. "A second time? No one's done that before."

"We'll see about that. Gary is going to fuck your pussy until you come."

She hid her smirk by looking down. That wasn't going to happen unless… She looked toward the sliding glass doors. The only way that would happen was if *he* came back on his rounds. And if he didn't? She rested her forehead on the footboard. She'd fake it. No reason to get sore for nothing. Besides, a part of her felt sorry for the woman. Yes, she was a submissive, but Adriana had to grit her teeth at the whole Dom/sub relationship.

The woman's tongue lapped against her clit, sending pleasing tingles up into her core.

Then again, it did have its advantages for her. She may not come, but she certainly planned to enjoy every sexual pleasure. And if the resort's mysterious security guard happened by again, she'd be ready.

Hunter McKade stalked away from the well-lit casita, his anger, always close to the surface, threatened to erupt. Why the fuck did he watch her every time? It wasn't as if he'd ever let himself experience that joy again, so why watch someone else have it? Self-directed fury tore through him, the hard-on in his jeans an annoyance.

He broke into a run up the hill toward the main building,

letting the resentment rush through his body. He pushed his muscles, ignoring the cold night air so similar to Afghanistan. Habit had him scanning the distance for the lights of smugglers making their way through the mountains.

The Arizona desert remained dark. No enemy to avoid, no landmine to watch for.

When he reached the building, he curved left at the dirt road down into the ravine, his cowboy boots with their special rubber-coated soles and heels gripped the rock-strewn path, allowing him to continue his sprint. He hit the bridge over the creek, his boots silent in the quiet night, keeping his presence hidden despite the turmoil inside.

The winding path up the ravine wall was steep, but he refused to slow. He focused on his breathing, the burn in his thighs, the blood pumping through his body. When he made it to the top, he finally slowed to a jog, circling the three-walled steel garage big enough to fit half a dozen Abrams tanks. As he approached the open side again, he stopped and stepped inside, flicking on the overhead lights.

The rose-colored bulbs gave a warm feeling to the metal structure, a false impression.

To bring his breathing under control, he paced between the rows of parked vehicles. Wintertime at a nudist resort in Arizona brought in a shitload of people. He studied each vehicle, a habit he'd obtained since returning home.

He snarled at his thought, barely keeping his fist from slamming into a four-door sedan. He had no home anymore. No home, no life, no reason to go on. So why the fuck did he?

He turned the corner and slowed to a stop. The second vehicle down, a red SUV of the same make and model as the one that used to grace his ranch, was parked there, laughing at him, taunting him with its pretty paint job and dent-free body.

Fisting his hands as his heart raced, he moved past it, focusing on the light switch. "Hold it together, Hunter."

Why? Why should he?

He turned off the lights and shut out the image of the vehicle. He stood there in the dark, his breathing labored all over again, his heart speeding beyond its legal limit.

Poker Flat. The staff here. That was why he had to rein himself in. They didn't deserve the havoc he wanted to wreak. He focused on his boss and her fiancé, Wade. They were good people who didn't care that he was screwed up from the inside out. More on the inside than what the bombs had done to his outside.

His heartbeat started to slow. Lacey, the bookkeeper, was sweeter than apple pie, and Selma's cooking was a step above delicious. Jorge, the stable manager, took care of the horses like they were his children.

His body calmed, and he strode from the garage, heading back toward the resort. With the eruption of chaos averted and the usual darkness settling into his psyche and taking hold, he couldn't decide which was worse.

As he crested the ledge of the ravine, his gaze swept the entire resort. First, to the shelf with the stables and the newly constructed western main street. The figure of Mac stepped out of the stable manager's office and headed toward the western town. She made her rounds like he did his.

His gaze swept to the other shelf with the main building and casitas. The light still shone from one in particular. His cock responded as the image of Adriana Perez having sex with three people forced its way into his head.

He made his legs move, taking him down toward the ravine bed. The resort's bartender was taking a risk being tied up by people she didn't know well. He shook his head as his instinct to protect surfaced once again. He wished he hadn't chosen law enforcement before and during the army. Now he couldn't stop the serve and protect instincts, even if he cared less about himself.

His feet took him to the guest casitas again. He willed himself to stop before reaching the lit one. Adriana could take care of herself. She had yet to call him to evict an unruly customer at the bar, though he'd heard from his boss there had been a few since he'd been hired in October.

Then again Kendra could have exaggerated. Adriana was not a big woman like Mac. She was of average build for a female, but with large breasts, a thin waist and a round ass that had many of the resort's guests looking twice. But it was far more than her salacious body, petite nose, full lips and laughing brown eyes that caused people to watch her. The woman oozed sex appeal.

The way she walked, how she spoke, even her mannerisms said she was interested in sex. She was the kind of woman his mother had always told him to steer clear of and he had, until now. Now *he* was the one good people needed stay away from.

The light from the casita beckoned him like the light after death. He found it impossible to resist.

A quiet voice caught his attention, his senses always alert. He stepped farther into the shadow of the casita made by the weak moon as an older couple came down the walking path. They were naked as expected, but what was odd was there was no sound of flip-flops. Everyone wore those in the desert.

As they drew closer to the casita Adriana was in, they slowed and he was able to see they were barefoot. With snakes and tarantulas about, that wasn't a smart move. He was about to make himself known when the woman pointed.

"See," she whispered. "That's Dominance and submission."

The older gentleman with bright-white hair and a large gut nodded. "That's what I thought. So where does the masochism and sadism come in?"

The white-haired lady shrugged her pudgy shoulders. "I don't know. I think that's if they use whips and chains."

"That makes sense." The two watched the scene inside the casita, both barely blinking.

Hunter's own curiosity made him impatient to step around the corner, but he determinedly held his position.

"Oh wow. Honey, look." The woman squeezed her husband's arm. "He just put his penis in that other man's butt."

The husband didn't respond right away, his gaze on something entirely different. He glanced at what his wife mentioned, then pointed. "And that woman is performing oral sex on Adriana even while the man's penis is inside her."

The wife pulled his arm. "We better go, I don't think she'd like us watching."

The husband didn't budge, but he did chuckle. "We're talking about Adriana. The woman who walks around the resort nude when she's not on shift. I think she would love us to watch."

"Oh, I think she's coming."

The husband didn't respond to his wife's comment. Instead,

they stood in silence as muffled sounds came from inside. When those sounds died down, the man had a hard-on.

The wife finally looked at him. "I'm ready now."

He grinned at her. "Me too. Let's go."

As the two ambled off, Hunter took a deep breath, confidant he'd made the right decision not to interrupt. But once they were out of sight, he stepped around the corner, this time careful to stay away from the light shining out of the sliding glass doors.

He expected to see Adriana untied and sitting on the floor recovering. He'd witnessed a number of nights when she didn't leave a sexual encounter until the sun threw a pink glow over the desert.

She wasn't untied yet. That bothered him. He'd only seen her tied once before and shortly after coming she'd been untied. Adriana would never be a submissive. A Dominatrix maybe, but never a submissive.

He watched the scene unfold inside. Adriana now knelt on the floor but her hands were still tied to the footboard. The other woman was on the bed, her legs spread wide, facing Adriana.

One of the men was missing, probably in the bathroom, but the other was arguing with Adriana. Hunter's gut tightened. This could get out of hand for her.

The man pointed to the woman on the bed. Adriana scowled at him, holding her hands up as far as they could go as she argued back. The man folded his arms and said something else.

Adriana shook her head, her chin coming up in defiance. The other man came into the room, a nasty-looking whip in his hand. Every muscle in Hunter's body came to attention. He curled his fingers into his palms. If this is what Adriana wanted, he'd hold his position, but if not…

He'd seen his fair share of kink while in the military. He'd even discovered his own captain with his dick stuck up the ass of one of his men. But it had been consensual and as far as Hunter was concerned, live and let live. He was in no position to judge anyone.

But he'd also seen rape and been prevented from interfering due to so-called "diplomatic relations," then been forced to bury the victim weeks later.

He narrowed his eyes at the scene before him, his weight already shifting to the balls of his feet. The dominant man now had the whip in his hand and pointed to the woman on the bed. Adriana lifted her tied hands again. The man raised the whip. She shook her head and spit on the floor.

He'd only seen her do that once, but she was furious at the time. He pulled the door handle as the whip came down.

Nothing happened. It was locked.

The impediment brought his rage to the surface. Picking up the stone planter at the edge of the patio, he threw it into the glass, his body coming through after it.

"Hunter!" Adriana's look of relief was all he needed to see.

He squelched his instinct to put down the enemy first. Holding on to his new reality by a thread, he pulled the switchblade from his back pocket and cut the rope binding Adriana's hands. Then he faced the two men. "You will leave this resort immediately."

Keeping his eyes on their surprised faces, he felt Adriana stand up behind him. "Do you want to press charges?"

Before she could answer, the man with the whip raised it and brought it down toward him.

Hunter lunged, grabbing the leather coil at the thong and ripped it out of the Dom's hands. He wrapped the whip around the man's neck, cutting off his air supply. "Adriana, do you want to press charges?"

The other man pulled at his arm, trying to loosen his hold as the dominant man struggled to breathe.

She stood next to him on his left not saying anything. The need to choke the life from the man took over his brain. He tightened the whip, his gut rejoicing at the gurgling sounds coming from the victim in his hands.

Something soft brushed against his shoulder. He stopped tightening at the movement. Adriana was there, a piece of his new reality. He wasn't allowed to kill.

"No." Her emotionless word, spoken softly as she shrugged and moved away, broke through his killing haze.

He released the whip and the man crumpled to the floor. Hunter kept his voice even. "You have one hour to vacate."

The other man knelt beside his companion, but Hunter turned his back on them. Keeping alert for an attack, he checked on Adriana, who had picked up her towel and slipped her feet into her flip-flops. She moved toward the sliding glass door naked, but hesitated to walk through the broken glass.

He stepped up next to her, glass crunching under his boots. "Allow me." Grabbing a towel from a nearby chair, he wrapped it around his arm and batted away the remaining glass sticking to the doorframe. When he finished, he dropped the towel and opened his arm in invitation.

Adriana nodded, as if having a busted window was a normal nightly occurrence, and sauntered through. He'd seen many women hold it together with bombs exploding yards away, but he'd never seen one walk away from a sexual assault without shaking uncontrollably or shifting in to a zombie-like trance as shock set in. Adriana appeared to be neither.

He looked back before stepping through. The two men were still on the floor, but the young woman with short blonde hair sat on the bed watching him, resentment glittering in her eyes.

"One hour." He turned and strode outside. He'd be back in an hour with Mac as backup, just in case the threesome decided to give him trouble. He wouldn't need her help, but she'd be pissed if she heard he'd handled the whole thing by himself.

Adriana headed up the path, her stride faster once away from the casita. He followed to make sure she arrived at her own place behind the main building unaccosted.

As they crested the plateau, she tripped. He grabbed her arm to keep her from falling.

"Thanks." She pulled her arm away, but not before he'd felt her shaking. She *had* been affected.

~~~~~

Adriana called herself three times a fool. She thought she was safe on the resort. That having Hunter and Mac patrolling the grounds meant she'd never have to worry about idiots, but she'd been wrong, lulled by the benevolent character of most nudists. *Most* being the key word.

She was freakin' shaking like a leaf when nothing had actually happened…thanks to Hunter. How he arrived at just the right time, she had no clue, but she was thankful. When he grabbed her arm though, she hadn't known he was behind her and it added to her shakes. Now he knew she was rattled and she hated that. He'd probably lecture her on choosing her bedmates. She was an expert at choosing sex partners. Usually.

She just made a slight error in judgment. She thought she could handle the Dom. Maybe she'd been just a little desperate for a night of sex when she'd accepted the offer to join them, her gut telling her the threesome would satisfy her better than the foursome. *Note to self: don't get desperate for sex.*

When she arrived at her casita, she opened the door and turned to thank Hunter again, but he was already in her doorway, filling it with his big body, his black clothing making him almost a part of the night. But he was solid and quiet and reassuring in a strange way.

She dropped her towel on her coffee table as if he always walked her home after a night of her having sex with whatever willing guests were up for it. "Thanks for your help back there."

He didn't say anything. Instead, he closed the door and flicked the switch that turned on the small lamp on an end table in her living room.

Half of her hoped he'd been turned on by the scene and wanted her in bed. The other half shivered at the deadly force he'd used on the Dom. To cover up her uncertainty, she moved into her kitchenette and washed her hands. Still, he didn't say anything. He just stood there, dressed all in black from his boots to his hat, taking up all the space in her living room. At least that's how it felt.

Shouldn't he be asking if she was okay? Duh, of course she was. Would he lecture her?

Hell, she didn't know him at all except that he watched her have sex every time she hooked up with guests and her body had come to depend on him watching in order to orgasm. Did he know she saw him or that he was the catalyst for her ecstasy?

She needed to get out of her own head. She opened the refrigerator, the cold air on her naked body making her step back. "Would you like a drink? I've got ice tea and water."

When he didn't reply, she closed the door and looked at him. He studied her house like he was profiling her or something.

"You don't talk much do you?"

The damn cowboy shrugged. Shrugged! "Well, I'm going to bed to get some rest. I need it after that close call. I'm sure you have to get back to your security duties."

He finally faced her. "Come here."

Her sheath tightened at his command, even as her mind rebelled. "Why?"

"Bring a warm washcloth."

"Now you just wait a minute. I've had just about enough of being told what to do tonight."

That had him moving, right for her. She squelched her instinct to run and instead pressed her ass against the cupboards. This was *her* casita. He had no right to…

CHAPTER TWO

He walked around her and pulled open the second drawer down to the right of the sink. Taking out a clean washcloth, Hunter turned on the faucet and wet it.

Hold on, how did he know where she kept her washcloths? "What are you doing?" That he wasn't interested in her was obvious. She was standing there as naked as the day she was born and he wasn't even glancing at her breasts.

"Turn around."

She faced him instead, one hand on her hip. "I asked you what you think you're doing?"

"I'm helping. Now turn around."

"Listen. Believe it or not I can—" Before she could complete her sentence, he whipped her around and settled the cloth on the back of her shoulder. At first she felt the warmth only, but then it started to sting…a lot. "Fuck, that hurts."

"He got you with the whip. It needs to be cleaned."

Holy shit, she'd forgotten. She'd been so angry when the Dom decided she should eat out his girl, Tina—not because she didn't want to make the woman come, but because she'd told him she was done. She'd even used the supposed "safe" word. Hah.

She hadn't even come a second time, but she'd faked it well. The Dom had just wanted her to submit. He'd been spoiled by his submissive.

Now, as the warm moistness soaked into her skin, the sting started to fade and she became acutely aware of how gentle Hunter was. She hadn't pegged him for gentle. Ruthless, like choking the air from the Dom's body, yes. Fast, in how he grabbed the whip right out of the Dom's hand. Quiet, as he walked behind her. Hell, she hadn't even known he was there until he caught her arm when she'd tripped. But gentle?

He took the cloth away and wrung it out in the sink. She watched as his strong hands squeezed the pink color from the cloth. Pink.

She snapped her head back and swallowed hard. She couldn't deal with the sight of blood. Not even her own. Vomit was fine. Broken bones bent awkwardly, no problem. All of which she'd seen as a bartender, but blood? Uh-uh. Her stomach started to roll.

She would not vomit and make an ass of herself. She would not.

Hunter clasped her left shoulder as he placed the warm cloth farther down her back, easing her tense muscles until the sting started again.

"Damn, how long is that scratch? What'd he have on the end of that thing, broken glass?"

"Knots."

"Knots? They must be into the "S" and "M" side more than they let on. Figures."

The warm moisture eventually eased the sting. This time when he took the cloth away to rinse it, she didn't watch.

When he reapplied the warm cloth, this time to her lower back, she gritted her teeth, not just because of the sting, but because she was pissed at the Dom, and herself, for getting into such a stupid situation.

"Why don't you want to press charges?"

Hunter's question, out of the blue, surprised her, but didn't jolt her as it was said in such a low, quiet tone that if it wasn't so desert-quiet around her casita, she'd have missed it.

She glanced over her shoulder at him, but could only see the brim of his hat. "Because it's not worth it. I was willingly tied. I knew he was a Dom. And there is always that little part about me being a former prostitute that would get in the way of any judgement in my favor."

"I was a witness."

"True, that would hold some weight, but they would still think I was asking for it and the Dom couldn't help getting carried away. Better to just forget it. As long as they leave." Her gut tightened at the thought the three could still be around come the morning. "You will make sure they leave, right?"

The cloth left her back and he stepped in front of her. "I promise. They'll be gone in less than an hour, even if I have to knock them out and carry them to their car." His metal-gray eyes were so intense with promise that she couldn't breathe.

She nodded and parted her lips to pull air back into her lungs. "Thanks."

He immediately returned to cleaning her back.

Where did Kendra find him? Everything about him was

intense, as if every aspect of him was taken to the eleventh power. For the first time since she could remember, she wanted to know more about a man. More than what was beneath his clothes.

"Stay here." His low tone, filled with command, caught her off guard.

But as he brushed by her and headed for her bathroom, she found her voice. "Now what are you doing?"

He wasn't in there long. He didn't even close the door. Then she heard the cupboard under her sink close and he strode out. Hell, the man moved like a snake, smooth, quiet and deadly. If she were a weaker woman, she'd shiver just watching him, but her interest was more of a sexual nature. The idea of going to bed with him, or anywhere else, took root and dug in deep.

"This will be cool, but it won't hurt." His voice behind her again had her redirecting her thoughts.

"What is it?"

"An antibiotic cream to stave off infection. When you go to bed, try to sleep on your stomach. If you have to, roll up a blanket and put it on both sides of you to keep you from rolling over. And don't wear anything to bed."

She looked over her shoulder at that. "I never do." She couldn't help the purr in her voice and was disappointed when he didn't look up from his task. The man must be made of stone. She'd been naked since he burst through the glass of the guest casita and he didn't seem affected at all. Maybe he didn't find her attractive?

She chuckled. Not possible.

"Is something funny?" His voice, though still low, sounded affronted.

"No, just laughing at myself and berating myself for my

stupidity. I should have gone with the swinging foursome." She bent a little, testing the feel of her wound. "It's probably good I got this scratch. It will remind me to be more careful next time."

Hunter spun her around to face him so quickly, it took her eyes a moment to focus and when they did she forced herself not to pull away.

"This was not your fault. Understand?"

She nodded, the intensity in his eyes reminding her of the efficiency with which he'd wrapped the whip around the Dom's throat.

"No woman deserves to be forced to do anything she doesn't want."

He clearly wasn't seeing her anymore and her curiosity grew. Time to lighten the conversation a bit. She winked. "It's pretty hard to find something I don't want."

He blinked, obviously not following and then his lip quirked, but he didn't say anything. Instead, he let go of her and screwed the cap back on the tube of cream. When he finished, he tipped his black hat slightly before turning and striding to the door.

She watched him, or rather his ass covered in black denim. When he opened the door and looked at her, she forced her gaze to meet his.

"Lock your door tonight."

"Got it." She moved forward, even as he pulled the door shut.

Turning the lock, she pulled the curtain aside to look out, but Hunter was gone. No surprise there.

She turned away and headed for the bathroom. Obviously, a shower was out, but she needed to clean up. Filling the sink with warm water, she grabbed the soap from the shower.

The night's activities flashed before her and her back started to throb. Dropping the soap into the water, she grasped both sides of the pedestal sink.

"What if he hadn't been there?" The fear she'd refused to acknowledge crawled its way back into her consciousness, bringing with it long-buried memories.

Adriana's hands tightened around the edges of the basin as her stomach threatened to regurgitate everything in it. Squeezing her eyes shut, she fought against the fear, the images of blood on the floors and walls, the sounds of screams piercing the afternoon idle.

Think of something else. Anything.

She opened her eyes, focusing on the brown of her irises in the mirror. Brown like whiskey, amaretto, scotch. She needed two bottles of scotch. How many bottles of gin did she have? At least one in the well, two in the cabinet. Were there any in the storage room?

She had to put in her order tomorrow with Lacey. She needed more limes. There were never enough limes. She had plenty of maraschino cherries, but she needed more swizzle sticks. And those cheap drink umbrellas. She'd been serving a ton of coladas lately.

Her breathing slowed as she focused on what she needed for the bar. Locking the fear and past back up where it belonged, she gazed at her reflection in the mirror and forced her fingers to relax around the sink rim. Tears had tracked mascara down her face and her tan skin looked blotchy.

"*Chica*, you look like hell."

~ ~ ~ ~ ~

Hunter sat on the edge of the desk in Kendra Lowe's office, waiting for her to arrive. His shift was over, but he wanted to tell her why he'd busted one of her casita sliders. If she balked that he'd over-reacted, he'd walk.

A tinge of regret at that prospect slinked through his anger, surprising him. He did feel more comfortable here than anywhere else, which said a lot since just being in his own skin was uncomfortable, like being forced to crawl under barbed wire that was two inches too low to the ground.

Footsteps coming down the hall had him listening. Cowboy boots. All staff wore them except the cook, but the stride was masculine. "Wade."

Wade halted just inside the doorway. "Good morning, Hunter. Not used to seeing you this late in the morning. Everything go okay last night?"

"Yes, but we had trouble." Technically, everything did go well. He took care of the situation.

"Shit." Wade strode in and slapped a piece of paperwork on his fiancée's desk. "When are the people in this area going to accept this place?"

"It was a guest."

Wade stared. "A guest?"

"They have been escorted off the property."

"That bad, huh? So that's why you're here, to tell Kendra. Hold on, let me get her. Last I saw, she was just pouring her first cup of coffee, but this should wake her up." Wade took out his phone and typed. "Come on, go through." He waited. "If I have to go—good. She should be here any minute now. Do you want some coffee?"

Hunter shook his head. He needed to get to sleep.

"I think I'm going to need another cup to hear this." Wade strode out.

Hunter listened to Wade talking to Lacey. He couldn't hear what he said, but he'd bet money he was letting Lacey know. Maybe even having her pull up a guest list. At least the man didn't ask him to explain the situation twice.

Footsteps quickly striding down the hall told him Kendra had arrived. As soon as she walked in the door, she took off her cowboy hat and dropped it on the desk. "Tell me."

He glanced at the doorway.

"Wade, come in here!" She shrugged out of her jean jacket and sat in her chair behind him, so he moved to stand next to the window. From the look on his boss's face, no one would think anything was wrong. She'd been a professional poker player and was an expert on hiding her emotions when she wanted to.

Wade came in, Lacey, the receptionist, trailing behind.

"Okay, spill." Kendra looked at him expectantly.

"One of the guests got carried away with some bondage and Domination last night. It went beyond consensual and I had to break the slider to stop it."

The silence in the room said far more than any gasp. Lacey, in her creamsicle sweater and white cowboy hat was the first to break the silence. "I just can't believe we would have any nudists here who would do such a thing. Who was it?"

He shrugged. "Casita Eight."

Lacey clasped her hands in front of her. "That was a threesome. The woman, Tina I think, was very submissive."

"It wasn't Tina." He waited.

Kendra finally spoke, her poker face failing as concern lowered her brow. "Adriana. Is she all right?"

"Yes, mostly. She can give you the details. I was patrolling the area. Luckily, the light was on and the curtains were open. I was able to stop it before it got too out of hand."

"Bastards." Kendra's hiss echoed everyone's sentiments, even his own.

"I had to break the glass to get in. They'd locked the door."

Wade shook his head. "I'm glad you were there at the right time."

Yeah, so was he. "I'm heading back to my place now. Do you need anything from me?"

"Does she want to press charges?" Kendra stood, her concern tinged with anger.

The way they all rallied around the bartender made him relax. This was a good place. "She told me she didn't."

"Those jerks are never coming back here." Lacey spun on her heel and left the room.

Wade grinned. "And I'll bet they won't be welcomed at any other nudist resort once Lacey gets on the network."

"As it should be." Kendra walked around her desk. "I'll talk to Adriana more about it when she comes in." She looked at him. "But she wasn't hurt?"

He fisted his hands and released them. "The door was locked. It took a second to break the glass."

Kendra's eyes widened as she opened her mouth, but Wade stepped up to her and pulled her against his side. "Thank you. I imagine you're tired. We'll take care of the door and Adriana."

He had no doubt they would. Tipping his hat in

acknowledgement, he left the office and headed for his casita, his body relaxing with his stride. He'd been at Poker Flat for four months and didn't interact much with the rest of the staff, mainly due to his hours, but also because of his preference. It reassured him that the staff rallied around their own. He'd made the right decision to accept a job here.

He strode down the dirt path behind the main building where the staff casitas were. He hadn't expected to fit in. His old high school buddy had placed him in three other jobs, but he hadn't been able to adjust, the lack of purpose to the position chafing at him.

Poker Flat was different. The resort needed him. That had been proved the very week he was hired on as security guard. It fit in well with his military police background. Plus, the night hours allowed him to be alone most of the time. The desert was like home after two tours in Afghanistan. The fact that people walked around with no clothes was a bonus—it meant they weren't hiding any weapons.

Burying his hand in his front pocket, he pulled his key ring out. As he stepped up to the door, he slowed. Someone was there. Covertly, he glanced to his left and right. There, near the corner of the house leading to the patio around back were footprints in the dirt. He palmed his keys to keep them quiet and moved to the side of the little house.

He glanced around the corner of his casita. No one was there. He scanned the ground. The footsteps led to his patio. Without hesitation, he crept toward his sliders.

Fuck, they were open at least an inch. He scanned his interior, but didn't see anyone inside from his vantage point, which left the entire east side of his living room unseeable. Carefully, he pulled his knife from his back pocket and exchanged it with the keys.

With weapon in hand, he threw open the slider and stepped in.

"You finally came home. I thought your shift ended over an hour ago."

Adriana sat on the love seat that came with the house. Her long, shapely legs in black cowboy boots, crossed, her short denim shorts frayed at the thighs, making her crotch all that more enticing. Her waist was bare but her substantial breasts were covered with a tight black leather vest zipped halfway up, showing a serious amount of cleavage.

When he raised his gaze, her smirk made promises it shouldn't and pure animal lust was obvious in her cinnamon-brown eyes.

"Shit, woman. I could have skewered you." He closed his knife and dropped it in his back pocket, his heart pumping extra hard as it came down fast from the adrenaline rush of catching someone in his place. "How did you get in here?"

Her lips formed an enticing pout. "Welcome to you, too."

He rubbed his face with one hand and strode to the kitchen. He needed sustenance. Opening the fridge, he grabbed a protein shake and unscrewed the top. As he took a swallow, he forced his body to calm. Between stifling his reflexes and her sex appeal, he was ready to lash out at anything. She was as sexy clothed as she had been naked.

He needed to focus on her face and what she'd been through last night. He brought the bottle down.

"You drink that stuff?" She squinched up her little nose. "I've tasted one of those. They're disgusting."

He raised the bottle in a toast. "Beats MREs." He took another swallow. The cool coffee-flavored liquid helped to relax his stomach.

"MR whats?"

He waved her off. "Never mind. What do you need, Adriana? I need to get some sleep."

Her gaze started at his boots and wandered over every inch of him, making it clear she wanted him. Shit, the woman was a Goddamn seductress.

She shrugged, breaking his concentration and he gulped down the rest of the shake.

"I came to make you breakfast. I thought it was the least I could do." She stretched her arm out across the back of the love seat, showing a tightly toned arm. "Granted, I'm not Selma, but since I'm guessing you don't get to eat much of her food either, I figure my skills should be enough."

He dropped the bottle into the trash. "Thanks, but I'm good. Shouldn't you be asleep yourself?"

She finally looked away.

Ah, he got it. "Nightmares."

Her gaze swung back to him, before she waved him off. "Over last night, hardly."

He shook his head. "No, not about last night."

Again she broke his gaze. "I just wanted to do something nice for you. I really appreciated your help."

He moved across the room to the slider and closed it, locking it. There was no sign of forced entry, so why was it unlocked? He turned to face her and found her standing. "How did you get in here?"

She pulled a skinny metal object from her back pocket. "I picked the lock. One of my old clients showed me how. I left it open for the fresh morning air. I love that it's still crisp. You might want to think about putting in a bar to hold it closed. It's safer that way."

He raised his eyebrow. "And do I need a bar here?" He'd found the place to be relatively safe, except for the occasional outside troublemaker and the guests from last night.

She sauntered up to him, leaning toward him as she lay her hand on his shirt. A whiff of sage and fresh linen filled his nostrils, causing his body to come alive against his will.

"Only if you need a bartender. I'm very good at tending bar."

Her hand felt warm, the first touch of another human he'd experienced beyond a handshake since coming to Poker Flat. That and his catching her when she tripped last night. He still remembered the softness of her skin and an urge to whip off his shirt so he could feel her hand caught him by surprise.

She gazed up at him beneath long black lashes, her eyes filled with erotic promises. "I can mix you up whatever you like. A little of this, a little of that." She raised herself up on her toes, leaning into him, her breasts just teasing his shirt and her breath wafting across the scruff on his chin. "Or do you like your pleasure as a shot, neat?"

Shot? Shot of alcohol? Fuck no. He stepped away quickly, turning his back on her as he strode to the door. Opening it, he looked at her. "I need sleep."

Her eyes went from wide with shock to narrowed in calculation within seconds. "Fine, cowboy. If you prefer sleep over pleasure, it's your choice." She grabbed up her black straw cowboy hat she'd left sitting on the love seat and sauntered toward him.

Didn't the woman know how to walk without moving her hips so much?

When she reached him, she stopped. "You know where to find me if you need me." Then she leaned forward and pressed her lips to his.

Hunter fought every nerve in his body to keep from responding. He didn't want his body to come alive. Reminders that he still breathed infuriated him.

When she didn't get a response, she plopped her hat on her head and scowled, but she didn't say a word, just shook her head and left.

He closed the door, resisting the urge to rip it off its hinges. Fuck. Now his body was tight with wanting as if it deserved something.

Stalking to the bathroom, he stripped, turned on the cold tap and jumped into the stream of water. "Fuck."

Adriana picked up her pace as soon as the door closed behind her. That cowboy was hiding a boatload of crap and she planned to find out what.

She headed straight for the main building. She had over two hours before her shift and she would put them to good use. It wasn't as if she could go back to bed. Freaking nightmares. Hunter's guess was too on the money. She would have been fine except for the blood on the cloth he used.

She moved her back experimentally as she opened the glass door of the "lodge" as she called it. The large one-story structure housed the reception area and offices, the dining room, kitchen, gathering room with giant stone fireplace and the indoor bar. All the wood, stone and stucco reminded her of a lodge she'd been to in the Sierras when one of her clients paid for a whole weekend of her company. That had been a particularly enjoyable time with a rather hunky client.

As she entered the building, she admitted Hunter's first aid had left her with just a slight twinge. She had no idea what her back looked like because she'd avoided her three-way mirror. If she was still bleeding, she didn't want to know.

She didn't look exactly "western" today which was the work uniform for the resort. All employees had to be dressed while on shift, not that hers started for a few hours yet, but she didn't plan to change. She'd worn her black leather zip-front halter, frayed jean shorts and black cowboy boots with a black straw cowboy hat. She called it her "biker –western" wear.

What she loved about working at the nudist resort was when she wasn't on the clock, she could strut around naked all she wanted. It definitely helped to procure invitations into guests' beds.

She slowed as she sauntered down the hall and into Lacey's domain. At least the tight black vest she wore would hide any stain. "Morning, Lacey." She moved to the coffeepot and poured herself a mug. She was wired from last night and her body was on a sexual high she got just from being around Hunter, but she needed something in her stomach.

When she heard no response from Lacey, she turned to look at her. "What's the problem, hon? Your jaw stuck?"

Lacey snapped her mouth closed and blinked. "What are you doing here this early?"

She shrugged. "Still weirded out. I'm guessing you heard."

Lacey nodded solemnly then took a step toward her. "I'm so sorry."

Adriana steeled herself as Lacey gave her a hug. The woman meant well, but the last thing she wanted was sympathy and the pressure on her back reminded her of her cuts.

Lacey finally stepped back. "Are you okay?"

She stuck her hand on her hip. "Don't I look okay?" She grabbed her earlobe with her other hand. "Don't you like these hoops?"

Lacey frowned. "That's not what I meant."

"I know, honey, but I'm fine." She chuckled. "You know it takes more than an unruly guest to bother me."

"I know, but you've never needed Hunter before."

Adriana wiggled her eyebrows. "Speaking of needing Hunter, what's his story?"

"Him, too?" Lacey threw her hands up. "I thought you didn't go for the good-boy types." She moved to the coffeepot and refilled her own cup.

"He's a good boy? That's not what my radar is telling me." Adriana took a seat at the small round table, ready to learn everything she could. "I can't believe I'm that off."

Lacey glanced through the doorway that led to the reception desk then took a seat. "Of course he is. He's a cowboy."

"Oh, I'll give you that, but he's more. Cowboys wear checkered button-down shirts and blue jeans. They don't wear all black *all* the time."

Lacey grinned. "Cole calls him Cash after Johnny Cash."

"Uh-uh, he's not a country singer either. Come on, girl. You've been around him a lot more than I have." *At least while clothed.*

Lacey took a sip of her coffee. "I haven't really spoken to him much because I work during the day. He's around more when you and Kendra are. The only time I ran into him at night was when he took away the guy that attacked my casita." Lacey grasped her cup with both hands. "Heck, I was so shaken up that someone could be so mad at me, I don't even remember if Hunter said anything. All I know is he appeared out of nowhere and took the guy away after Cole caught him."

Sounded like Hunter was good at appearing out of nowhere. She leaned back in her chair and held Lacey's gaze. "But you know a lot more about him because you have his personnel file. Tell me."

"Come on, Adriana. You know I can't release that information. Those files are private."

She didn't stop staring at Lacey. She wanted to know. It had been four months of watching for the man's black boots so she could get off. Now he'd broken her faceless fantasy, and being close to him triggered a craving inside that far surpassed her need for sex.

She didn't question it. She never did. Life was about following cravings. She was convinced they existed to help people enjoy life, if they'd only listen to them.

Lacey shook her head. "No. It's against policy." Her stern look crumbled. "I can't, I'm sorry."

Adriana looked at her sideways. "I trust you to balance my checkbook for me, but you won't trust me with a little information?"

Lacey was a sweetheart, but she was also a good girl, though not above manipulating people to get her way on occasion.

"Why don't you just ask Hunter yourself?"

She snorted. "Because he isn't exactly the talkative type."

"There is that." Lacey took another sip of coffee and her gaze turned shrewd. "Why do you want to know about Hunter? It's not like you need to know anything about a man before sleeping with him."

"Sleeping wasn't what I had in mind." She winked.

Her friend looked seriously troubled.

"What?"

"I don't think it's a good idea."

"Why? Is there something about him I should know? If so, you better tell me."

Lacey took a sip of coffee before responding. "I just don't think this is a good match."

She rolled her eyes. "I don't want to date him. I just want to have sex with him."

"Oh, I don't know. It feels…"

"Feels what? Spit it out."

"I think you should ask Kendra. She interviewed Hunter. She was very thorough in hiring her security guards *this* time."

Now that sounded promising. "Fine, if my supposed best friend can't help me then I guess I have to go over her head."

Lacey's face fell. "That's not fair. You know I want to."

Adriana winked. "Yeah, I do. Just had to give you a hard time for stonewalling me."

"I'm not—"

She laughed. "You're too easy, hon."

Lacey leaned back and checked the reception desk. "Oh, someone just came in." She stood, coffee mug in hand. "I have to go. Are we good?"

She nodded. "We're good. Go. Make someone happy."

"That's my job." Lacey beat a quick exit.

"And you do it so well, sweetie." Adriana took her half-finished coffee with her and meandered her way into Kendra's office. It was empty, but since the door was open, it meant her boss would be back.

She sat in the chair opposite Kendra's desk. A file cabinet tucked into a corner caught her eye. Only important papers would be in Kendra's office…like personnel files? She looked toward the door and listened for footsteps. All was quiet except for a muted conversation between Lacey and their new guest. What could it hurt?

She started to rise than flopped back into the chair. She'd be out on her ass in about ten minutes if she was caught. Since when was she willing to risk her job over a man? *Hell, Adriana, get a grip on yourself.*

Kendra was all about giving her staff a second chance by hiring them, but she refused to offer a third chance. Old Billy, the former wagon and golf cart driver, was proof of that. He'd been a functioning alcoholic until he wasn't anymore and then he got the axe. Yeah, it was a bit more than that, but the fact remained, Kendra wouldn't bend on the subject of another chance.

Adriana sighed. She had a good gig here. She wasn't going to lose it because of her curiosity over a—

Footsteps coming down the hall convinced her she'd made the right decision. When they stopped at the doorway, she let her head fall back. "Hey."

Kendra came in carrying a clipboard and placed it on her desk before sitting on the edge of it. "Are you okay?"

She held the coffee cup up. "Good enough. Got my caffeine."

"No, I mean how did they hurt you? Hunter said things got carried away."

That was one way of putting it. "Yeah, they did a little, but he showed up just in time."

Kendra shook her head. "He may have showed up, but he said he had to bust through the slider. That's heavy-duty glass rated to stand up to haboobs. It couldn't have shattered very quickly."

"So that's why it looked like sections of a giant spider web. Actually, he broke that sucker pretty damn fast."

Kendra crossed her arms. "Spill."

Adriana looked at the open door. Lacey might love sexy lingerie, but she didn't need to hear this.

Her boss caught the hint and moved to close the door. Then she sat in the other chair in front of her desk. "Okay. What happened?"

Adriana explained the final scene only. No need for Kendra to know everything that led up to the whipping.

Of course, Kendra didn't show any emotion at first. Adriana had noticed that when her boss was angry, upset, or frustrated, her poker mask reappeared. At least she'd become good at showing her emotions when she was excited, happy, or having fun. That and when she looked at Wade. It was strange seeing tough Kendra looking all googly-eyed at her man.

Finally, the emotion revealed itself and it wasn't pretty. Kendra was spittin' mad.

"Show me."

"What?"

"I want to see what damage was done."

Adriana shifted in her chair. She didn't care about stripping, but what if her cuts had seeped into her vest? Only one way to find out. If they stuck, she'd know, plus the leather vest was black. There'd be no blood stains even if she did look at it. "I didn't know you were that kind of girl." She smirked.

"Nice try. Now stand up, turn around and take off your top."

Adriana smiled as she rose. "You wouldn't believe the number of times I've heard those exact words. They trigger my horny side."

"Adriana, you don't have another side. Now stop stalling."

She barked a laugh at her boss and turned her back. Unzipping the vest completely in half, she let it drop down, but held it in her hands.

The office was quiet. No gasp, so that was a good thing. She didn't really want to be disfigured by a simple whip, even if the asshole had used knots. There were knots and then there were knots. Usually whips for sex play weren't set up to scar—leave marks, yes, scar, no. Doms liked their subs pretty.

A sudden sympathy for the girl Tina rose, but she squelched it. The woman had chosen the Dom for whatever reason. "So?"

"You can put your vest back on."

She turned and faced her boss. "Do I have to?"

Kendra looked at the clock. "Actually, no. You still have almost two hours before work. Maybe you should go get some rest."

She carefully pulled the vest back on, but didn't zip it. "Why? Is it that bad?" Her gut sank at the thought her back would be marred for life just because she'd been stupid. Kendra had much worse scars, so she really should count herself lucky.

"It looks like it's healing already. Who treated it?"

"Hunter. Do you think I'll have scars?"

Kendra shook her head. "I doubt it. Besides, your front is much more enticing to men than your back."

She grinned. "I'm not so sure. I had this one guy who just loved my booty. He couldn't get enough of it."

Kendra held up her hand. "Please, too much information."

Adriana laughed. "Since when?"

"Since—"

A knock on the door stopped the conversation fast.

"Sorry, Ms. Lowe." Andrew, their new wagon driver, stepped in, gripping his cowboy hat in both hands.

The lanky twenty-year-old had the beginnings of one handsome man. Adriana had thought about offering to teach him a few things in the bedroom he might not already know, but she'd hadn't had a chance yet.

"Andy, what is it?" Kendra stood.

Adriana joined her, facing Andy. His worried expression changed as his gaze moved to her open vest. She gave him her best seduction smile, but he didn't move his eyes from the inside outline of both her breasts. She was good with that.

"Adriana, zip up." Kendra waved her hand in front of Andrew's eyes. "You came in here for a reason. Could you think with your other head and tell us why?"

The man actually blushed before his memory returned. "Yes, it's Ms. Perez's car. I'm not sure, but I think someone was in it."

"What?" This had better be a bad joke.

Andrew nodded. "I just got back from bringing the Sandersons down. They had a lot of luggage, so it took a while to unload." He grimaced. "I'm not sure. But I know how you are always careful to lock your doors because you leave stuff in there."

"Yeah, so? I have a mess in my car. It's not like I use it that often living here with Selma's great cooking and guests free for the taking. Why? Is my car clean now?" She squelched her smile, only because the young man appeared very concerned.

He flushed again. "Well, no, miss, but I noticed the doors were unlocked when I drove up there. I didn't notice it when I came in this morning, but it could be because I didn't turn the lights on and when I just drove up now, the sun was shining in there, lighting the whole place up."

"Motherfucker." Adriana ignored Andrew's stunned expression. "Take me up there."

Kendra grabbed her arm. "Hold on. What are you thinking?"

"I'm thinking that Dom from last night got pissed he had to leave the resort and damaged my car somehow."

"Why? Did you tell him you drive a yellow convertible Camaro?"

Did she? "I have no idea. No wait. I haven't talked about my car all week. Damn, I'm slipping."

Kendra let go of her arm. "This could be a totally unrelated incident. If we're experiencing more vandalism, they could have chosen your car because it stands out like an oasis in the middle of a desert. Or you could have simply forgotten to lock your doors. When was the last time you used it?"

That was easy to remember. She'd gone into the city to try out a real sex swing before plunking down money online. "Four days ago."

"Okay, so let's go up to your car and see if anything is missing or damaged. If not, you just forgot to lock it."

She didn't forget. She may not be the neatest person on staff, but she always locked her car. That Camaro was her baby. She'd never loved anyone, but she damn well loved that car. "Lead the way."

Kendra motioned Andrew out of the room. "I hope we don't have to call Detective Anderson again. I had really hoped the residents of the area had finally accepted our nudist resort. We haven't had an incident here since last fall."

Adriana frowned. "Maybe not here, but there was plenty of excitement at the Last Chance Ranch. Between the Christmas and New Year's Day shootings, I'll bet he's still doing paperwork."

Andy put the tan golf cart in motion.

"I forget, it's all a matter of perspective." Kendra grinned. "At least on Poker Flat, I've been the only one to use a gun."

"So far." Adriana met Kendra's surprised look with a promise of her own. If that Dom had damaged her car, she was taking her Smith and Wesson out of retirement and shooting the man's ass.

CHAPTER THREE

Hunter rode in the sedan, his eyes constantly scanning the road ahead. This was stupid. The general he guarded had insisted on being taken by land to the base, but there were no armored sedans at the air field. One hour and they would have been in a safe helicopter. It wasn't as if it was an emergency.

General Rendez talked nonstop in the back seat to Major Jackson. Hunter had learned to tune out the jaw flapping of the higher ups. His job was to protect them, not nose around in their business, besides, he was pretty sure their business would nauseate him.

This second tour in Afghanistan was nothing like the first. Before he felt like he was accomplishing something, helping knock down terrorism and protecting bases where they brought in the wounded.

But he'd been promoted. Shit. It felt like a demotion to him. Guarding the movers and shakers of the army around a country that didn't even function as a country was a lesson in futility in his opinion. But what did he know? He was only Military Police.

But he did know how to survive and keep his charges alive.

The tiniest glint on the hill up ahead had his adrenaline kicking in. "Stop!"

"What? I can't stop. We're in the middle of nowhere." His driver, a man he'd never met that he now looked at with suspicion, kept moving forward.

"I said stop." He slammed his foot on top of the brake, bringing the sedan to a sudden halt. Swearing in the back was nothing but muffled sound to him.

He saw the flash as the mortar was sent. Fuck, they were dead. "Get out of the car!" He jumped out and threw open the back door. Pulling the general out, he pushed him ahead of him, away from the vehicle. The silence in the air made everything slow down as he pushed his muscles harder. The explosion shook the ground simultaneously with the concussion of air that picked him up and swept him forward.

Heat, pain and desperation sliced through his body. Then there was nothing.

Voices speaking Dari brought him to. Did he want to wake up? No. Yes. He had to get home to Julie. He had to live. The body beneath his own was warm. He had to protect her. What was Julie doing here? She was supposed to be home. His hand was wedged beneath him. If he could just reach his sidearm.

The voices grew louder. He wasn't sure if it was because they drew closer or his hearing was coming back online. Didn't matter which. He had to protect Julie. Wiggling his fingers, he felt every one of them. He moved his hand slowly to his side, hoping his M9 was still in its holster. His M4 was torn from his hand in the blast. His fingers grasped the cold metal of the Beretta's hilt. Confidence powered through him. He had a gun.

The voices grew louder. Arguing. Only two. That's what sucked here. So few could do so much damage. But he could take out two. Then he had to get Julie to the hospital. Or was she already there? Images of her in a hospital bed flashed across his vision. He must still be dazed from the explosion. Didn't matter. His training said take down the enemy and worry about wounded when the threat was eliminated.

A shout as the two men found the driver proved that man's innocence. Too bad he hadn't stopped out of range.

Hunter slit open one eye. Fuck, that's as far as it would go. One of the enemy walked around the wreckage, his weapon ready.

He only had one shot and it all depended on pushing himself up and swinging his arm around. He didn't even know if he could move, but if he went slow, he was dead anyway. Then what of Julie?

Her sweet smile, big eyes and flawless white skin that she swore she had to moisturize every day back in Arizona, blocked his vision for a moment. He had to get back to her.

No, he had to save her. Confusion swept through him and his head started to throb. He needed to focus.

The enemy drew closer. He waited. Watching for the telltale sign the man had relaxed. Not yet. The enemy kicked his boot. It didn't hurt too bad, which meant he still had his legs. It certainly felt that way.

Then the enemy kicked the leg beneath him. Anger boiled inside, pushing him to the edge. He couldn't let this man hurt Julie. She was his reason for living, for getting home to their ranch outside of Tucson.

Then he saw it. The loosened hand as the M16 dipped down toward the ground.

He pushed his torso up with his left hand as his right swung and pulled the trigger. The enemy went down.

His brain rejoiced as he collapsed on Julie. Darkness threatened as the thumping in his head increased, mixing with a yell and the pounding of feet.

He wanted to give in, but a groan from beneath him forced him to push away the black and embrace the hammering in his head. He opened his eye as the enemy pulled his gun up to his hip.

No fucking way.

He'd fallen on his arm so he cocked his wrist and shot just as the first bullets whizzed toward him. The enemy fell at the same time the burn of bullets pierced his leg and a yell from beneath him told him where the others had landed.

"No!" Julie was hit! She had to live!

His body jerked hard and he woke soaked in sweat. "What the fuck?"

Hunter blinked, focusing on the ceiling fan above him and the sunlight glinting off it. He wiped at his face with one hand. He wasn't supposed to have the nightmares during the day.

He threw off the blanket and swung his legs over the side of the bed. Leaning his elbows on his knees, he cradled his head. Just when he found a routine, his brain screwed him up again.

This one was new. He'd never dreamed his late wife was the general he'd saved. Too bad he didn't do drugs because they couldn't mess with his head any worse than it already was.

Standing up, he strode naked to the bathroom to take a piss then walked into the kitchen. He was starving. Adrenaline rushes in dreams demanded as many calories as the real thing.

Opening the fridge, he scanned the shelf of protein shakes. He had to admit, Lacey was efficient. But he needed real food.

Pulling the lunch meat drawer open, he grabbed the pound of sliced roast beef. He'd prefer a steak, but he didn't want to take that kind of time. He needed a lot more sleep. He glanced at the clock on the microwave. Shit. It was only one in the afternoon.

He dropped the beef on the counter and pulled out the casserole dish still half filled with the macaroni and cheese he made the day before. He mixed that up and stuck it in the microwave.

As the timer ticked down, he ripped open the roast beef and took a slice at a time and chewed. The primitive flavor of the pink meat permeated his mouth and soothed his brain. When the microwave rang, he pulled the dish out and set it on the stove top. Grabbing a spoon, he shoveled in a hot, cheesy portion.

Now *that* was comfort food. He focused on the flavors as they moved over his tongue. The tangy saltiness of the pasta and the course rawness of the meat. When he was finished he felt better, or rather his stomach felt better. His mind kept wanting to go back to the dream.

How the fuck was he supposed to sleep if he was going to dream again? Wrapping what was left of the meat, he stuffed it back in the drawer and placed the casserole dish in the dishwasher.

Then he sat on the stool at the counter with a bottle of water. He needed to force his mind to think of something else like they'd taught him. Anything.

Adriana's naked body as she walked into the light of her own kitchen emerged. The woman was sex on two legs, a dirty magazine centerfold/porn star/temptress in one. Every boy's and man's wet dream, but even better. She was exotic and beautiful and sensual naturally, like she'd been born to pleasure a man.

His cock hardened as he kept his focus. So what? No need to keep the sucker at bay now. She wasn't here. He indulged his fantasy.

She wouldn't need a bed. She'd want something down and dirty. She'd be happy to sit on this very counter, spread her legs and let him eat her out. No guilt. No commitments. No attachment beyond sex. His hand found his stiff cock and he started to rub it back and forth.

He could imagine her dusky skin changing to a dull pink at the lips between her thighs. He could lick every pale spot while being surround by her scent. He'd noticed it when he walked her home. It was like the desert at night, cool, crisp, fresh.

She'd grasp his head in her hands, urging him on, moaning loudly, free of all inhibitions. She wouldn't care who heard or who saw. Shit, she'd be happy to have an audience. They could invite the whole resort.

His hand stilled. Not like Julie. She enjoyed their intimacy, preferably in the dark, her tiny moans eeking out to tell him she enjoyed his touch.

He shook his head. He wasn't worthy of Julie anymore. She was gone. She wouldn't like who he'd become. He wasn't the cowboy hero she'd fallen in love with. He'd been so green, idealistic, thinking he could make a difference, first in their town and then for his country.

But he couldn't even save his own wife.

The dream edged into his psyche, threatening to take over again. "No."

His own voice cut it off. Dark skin, long black hair, breasts with large, dusky areolas and thick nipples. He could do that.

He could take Adriana anywhere. He turned as he grasped his ball sac and rolled them. Sitting on his stool, he gazed out at the patio, in the shade at the moment, the wood railing the perfect height for bending her over. He could envision her stomach across the top as he held her hips and sank into her wet and ready pussy. The glide would be spectacular.

Her sheath would contract around him, an expertise he was sure she had. He'd watched her so many nights. Not because he planned to, but on patrol he'd see the light and check to make sure all was okay. She was inside with at least two, maybe more, partners.

Her smile sultry even as someone pounded into her like he wanted to do. Her eyes bright with excitement, her every movement a dance of sexuality and enjoyment. She would laugh, her pleasure too much to contain and he could hear it.

He'd been drawn in like a man being tempted to the dark side. He snorted. He'd been living on that side since his first tour, he just hadn't realized it.

He always stepped forward, wanting to be closer to hear her orgasm as her body shook and her mouth opened with her scream.

But if he had her, it would just be the two of them. Two who lived better in the dark where their sins were less obvious. He could have her to himself, right there over the railing.

"More," her throaty voice would demand.

He could grip her hips and slide in and out, the tension fluctuating as she spurred him on. Pumping faster, he'd fill her every time to the brink, his balls slapping against her as she panted and moaned until screaming, her sheath contracted around him, milking his cock for all it was worth.

"Argh." The release of his come as it squirted onto the tile floor unwound his tension and freed his mind. He slowed his hand, holding a bit of pressure on his happy dick. "Nice job."

Finally letting go, he pulled paper towels from the holder and wet them to clean himself off. Trashing them, he grabbed another bunch and cleaned up the floor. Keeping his mind on the relief he felt, he returned to his bedroom and sprawled across the bed.

~~~~~

Adriana poured another round of shots. "That's it, folks. Going to have to close up now."

A chorus of whines from the four swingers followed her pronouncement.

"Ah, come on, Adriana. It's only one. The n-night is young."

She eyed the petite blonde with enhanced breasts. Patti was her name. "True, but I can't keep the bar open with only four customers. If you want, I can charge a bottle of tequila to your account and you can take it back to your casita."

"Oh, I like that idea. Do it."

She added the bottle of high-end tequila and handed it over. "There you go. Enjoy the rest of your night."

"Would you like to join us?" The blonde's husband, Steve, gave her a wink.

"You know I would, but I still have a lot of work to do. Need to add to my liquor order after all you guys drank and that goes out tomorrow."

Patti toasted the air with the bottle. "If you change your

m-mind and want to come over later, we're in casita number four." She giggled, finding that funny.

Patti was obviously already feeling a little too good. Adriana smiled. "Good to know."

As the foursome made their way down the path from the outdoor bar, she pulled the final shot glasses from the ironwood top and washed them in the scrubber.

She didn't have to close the bar. She could have kept it open until two, but she was tired. Three hours of fitful sleep had not been enough. Then added to that the news about her car, even though nothing had been missing, and she was wrecked. She was bound to drop more than a beer glass if she continued to tend bar and she hated cleaning up glass. The chances of being cut were too high.

She flicked the scrubber off and turned out the lower bar lights. She'd been surreptitiously cleaning up for the last hour, ready to call it a night.

Usually, she would jump at the chance to join a foursome, but being tired meant she couldn't judge the two couples well enough to know for certain it was safe. They probably were, but it was even more than that.

Wiping her hands on a bar towel, she grabbed it up and two others and threw them on the floor. That would remind her to pull out clean ones tomorrow afternoon.

She flipped the switch on the upper bar lights and walked toward the pool. Usually she took a dip on the nights she wasn't otherwise occupied after work, but she felt too tired for even that.

The moon was shining brighter, showing at least three quarters, making the area look like another dimension. Yeah, right.

She plopped down on a lounge chair and toed off her boots. She could probably sleep right here she was so tired, but the moonlight might keep her awake. Still, it felt good to get off her feet.

Between the whip last night and the shock at seeing her car mysteriously unlocked, it had been a rough one. Too bad she couldn't soak in a nice hot bath. She could, but that meant she'd have to run it, which would take far too long.

She glanced at the hot tub. That could work.

But she didn't move. Not a single muscle. There had been no damage to her car and everything she had in there was still there. Kendra was sure she'd just left it unlocked. But she hadn't. She always locked her car twice, just to be sure. It was habit.

She loved that car. It wasn't anything truly expensive or special but it was to her. Being able to buy it had been her first goal for herself when she'd joined the bordello in Sparks, Nevada. She'd been so naïve, but her looks and personality had made her one of the three most sought after girls at Mrs. B's.

To be truthful, she could have bought four of those cars, but it wasn't the same. Her baby was hers, but it was getting old. Maybe it was time to change the color. Maybe lime green. She grinned. Lacey would be horrified.

"You closed early." Hunter's voice came out of nowhere.

Her heart raced at being surprised and with the knowledge he was near. He was the reason she wasn't anxious to join a group tonight. She wanted *him*. She scanned the edges of the pool deck and found him, or rather the shadow of him at the opposite corner. "Crap, you're quiet. You almost gave me a heart attack."

He walked toward her, skirting the pool, but the moonlight hitting his cowboy hat kept his face in shadow. Damn, that was hot.

"I wanted to make sure you were safe."

She liked that. That polite cowboy part of him drew her as much as his silence did and the underlying danger in the way he moved. No one moved like that unless they were hiding something.

It was weird. She didn't even know if he was built. He was certainly big enough to have muscle under all his clothes, but the black material hid everything. For all she knew, he had a beer belly and flabby thighs.

He stopped about three feet from her. Just his presence, standing over her, had her nipples hardening. What the hell was wrong with her? "I think I'm safe. Why?" She sat up straight. "Did the Dom and his entourage try to come back?"

"No." The smooth sound of his voice in that one word calmed her like nothing could.

Now that made no sense. How could his voice both excite and relax her? She must need sleep. "I was just resting before heading to bed. No, that's not true. I was about to fall asleep right here. I'm wiped."

He didn't say anything, just stood there silent and dark, darker than the night. A shiver of excitement swept up her spine. He was Batman. She giggled. Freak, she must be really tired. She was losing it. "I guess I should go back to my casita. Could you give a girl a hand up?"

She stretched out her arm, hoping he'd take her hand.

He did and anticipation rumbled low in her belly. She was ready to purr. Then he pulled her toward him and she couldn't resist. As she stood, she leaned into him, grasping his shoulder. A very muscular shoulder. "Thanks." She forced herself to let go.

"I'll walk you home." His words, so simple, sent excitement tittering through her veins.

"Thanks. Whoa, wait. I need my boots." Stepping away from him, she shoved her feet in her cowboy boots and groaned. "I've spent far too many hours on my feet today. I much prefer being on my back." She winked at him, but couldn't tell if he caught it. His face was shadowed by his hat, except his lips and scruff, which were illuminated by the moon and they didn't move an inch.

He took a step back and opened his arm for her to precede him. That was terribly cowboy of him. Instead, she hooked her arm in his. "Okay, I'm ready, in so many ways."

She wasn't sure, but it felt like a tendon or something in his arm moved at her comment. It was so blasted hard to tell when he stayed silent and simply started walking. What she *was* sure of was that the arm beneath her own was rock hard and that had her mind warming already.

"So did you hear someone broke into my car?"

"No." He didn't even hesitate, keeping his stride short to accommodate her.

"They did. I think it was the Dom from last night, but I couldn't find anything taken or damaged. Kendra thinks I just forgot to lock my car. No way, Jose. That car is my baby. I lock it up good and tight every time." It still pissed her off that Kendra didn't believe she'd locked it. She wasn't so old she forgot stuff like that. She was thirty-two. In her sexual prime.

They took a few more strides before he spoke. "I'll check on it."

Those simple words that said he believed her had her anger dissipating. He certainly didn't say much, but what he said was the right thing. "Thanks."

They walked in silence, but it wasn't a comfortable one. She wasn't sure he was ever comfortable. She didn't like it. "Correct me if I'm wrong, but I'm guessing you didn't tell your mommy when you were a five-year-old that you wanted to grow up to be a security guard on a nudist resort. Right?"

This time she definitely felt a reaction in his arm. If she could see his mouth, she would bet money his lips quirked just a smidge.

"Right."

She waited, but this time she felt as if he were laughing at her, making her wait on purpose. It kind of turned her on. "So what did you do before you came here?"

"I killed people."

Any lightness she'd felt disappeared with those three words. "Cop?"

He grunted. "Military police."

So he was a veteran. His silent walk, the way he moved like a snake all coiled up and ready to strike. It fit. She didn't know one iota about the military. She'd never even had a client who'd been in the military. Probably because women just loved a man in uniform. Those guys didn't need to pay for it.

She should stick to what she knew but since when did she do what she should? "I thought I felt some muscle under these clothes. I'd really like to see it some time."

Did his step hesitate just a second there? She couldn't be sure. Now she had the urge to pull him into her casita, strip him of his black clothing and turn on every light she had. Even the old lava lamp she'd won in Reno.

As they reached her door, he pulled his arm out from her grip. She turned and faced him, wishing now her light was on outside. *Note to self: leave light on twenty-four hours a day from now on.* "I'd invite you in for a drink, but really what I'd like is a lot more than that."

"I don't drink." Hunter's tone was downright frigid.

Hmm, that hit a nerve. "I doubt that. I bet you drink water and orange juice and I know you drink that disgusting protein stuff."

"I'm on patrol."

"Right, of course." There was no way she'd get him into her bed while he was working. That was his police side. "Oh, you said you would look at my car. Do you need the keys? I locked it again this afternoon."

"Yes."

She waited for him to elaborate, but that appeared to be it.

Shrugging, she pulled her keys from her back pocket. She unlocked the door to her casita then handed him her key chain. "If you get a break, you know where to find me. And if you just need a little activity before going to sleep in the morning, don't hesitate to drop by." She gave him her most sultry smile, making it perfectly clear what kind of activity she was proposing.

He took the keys from her without even touching her hand then tipped his hat and turned away.

Just like that? He disappeared into the moonlit desert as if he'd never been there. What the hell?

Stepping inside her casita, she flicked on the light and dropped down on her couch to toe off her boots.

She must be losing her sex appeal or something. Either that or the man was made of stone. She stilled. What if he'd damaged his goods in the military? "Crap, that would suck."

Was that why he watched her get off? Did men like that want to watch? Hell, she didn't have a clue. She didn't even care why he watched as long as he did. That was pretty selfish of her.

She lay across her couch, too tired to move another foot. Now if he was there, she'd find her second wind, but he'd moved along. Unzipping her vest, she let her breasts breathe.

Making herself come would take more energy than she had, so she pulled the Mexican blanket from the back of her couch and spread it over herself against the chill and closed her eyes.

Maybe she could dream about having an orgasm instead... with a fully functioning Hunter.

Hunter continued his patrol around the staff casitas, walking off the sexual tension he felt whenever he was near Adriana. He wasn't surprised by it. In fact, he welcomed it. Her blatant sexuality made an excellent distraction.

He should thank her and he probably would eventually. When he was ready. In the meantime, she'd given him another distraction. Her vehicle.

Hunter strode toward the other side of the resort. Pulling out his cell phone, he flashed the area twice then put it away. The cell phone signal booster Kendra had installed worked only half the time, so he and Mac never completely depended on the phones.

Mackenzie Rivers stepped out from behind the Old West town and strode toward him. The woman was over six feet tall and in better shape than some of the men he'd served with. She kept her hair pulled back in a tight bun and with the weather still cold, wore dark-colored sweats and black sneakers. He didn't know what her story was, but she took her job seriously and that's all he cared about.

"What's up?"

He jerked his head in the direction of the guest casitas. "I need to take some time up at the garage. You want to cover the guest side too for a while?"

"Sure, unless you need me at the garage as well."

"No."

She stared at him a moment. "Something up there I should know about?"

"Don't know yet." It could be Adriana forgot to lock her car, but he wasn't going to put anything past the guests he'd kicked out last night. By the time he and Mac had reached their casita, they were gone. When he jogged up to the garage to make sure they'd left, he'd seen their tail lights down the dirt road.

They walked together toward the fork that split the resort in half.

"How's Adriana?" Mac's question derailed his thoughts.

"Hard to know. She seems fine. I think she blames herself."

"She shouldn't." Mac's voice changed. There was a guttural tone to it.

He stopped at the top of the ridge, his eyes scanning the casitas below. Only one was lit. Probably the foursome from the bar. "Be sure and check the lit casita. I escorted Adriana home when she got off, but since I turned down her invitation, she may go out again."

Mac raised an eyebrow then nodded. "Will do. Flash if you need help."

"Right." He headed down the path to the bridge, but once across, he jogged up the other side of the ravine. Kendra had given him and Mac golf carts, but they rarely used them. There was nothing like being on foot for catching people doing something they shouldn't.

The last catch had been a couple who were doing it on Adriana's bar. They'd been embarrassed he'd caught them, so they weren't Adriana's type. He caught plenty of guests having sex in public places of the resort, but if food or drink was served on the surface, he drew the line and left a note. Luckily, most of the nudists knew better.

As he came into the garage, he stopped. Listening to the night sounds, he catalogued every one. The scampering of a desert rat. The winged whisper of a late-night bat. A coyote off in the distance. No human sounds.

He didn't flick on the overhead lights. They would light up the whole desert north of Carefree Highway. Instead, he pulled out his mini-LED flashlight and clicked it on. Adriana's car was always parked in the back corner where staff kept their vehicles. It didn't take long to find it.

He had to give her credit. Choosing a yellow Camaro convertible instead of a red corvette definitely kept her from becoming a cliché. He'd bet a hundred bucks any cop that pulled her over was offered a blowjob if he let her off with a warning.

He shook his head. Julie would have simply cried with mortification. He froze. Where the fuck had that come from?

Refusing to go down that road, he focused on the Camaro, the flashlight reflected off the bright paint, lighting up the area.

The easiest way to break into a car without making it look like a crime occurred was to use a slim jim. He'd used that particular instrument more times than his gun when he'd been an officer in Oro Mesa. He shined the light on the window near where the locking mechanism would be.

There. His body tensed at his find. The lightest of scrapes along the window ridge could be made out. He followed the spot to the window. It was obvious the desert dust had been disturbed, showing the perpendicular marks of a slim jim.

The spurt of elation that came with finding a crime had been committed woke his brain as if it'd been asleep. The scratch and dust disturbance probably wasn't obvious during the day or with the lights on, but the darkness revealed a lot.

Adriana had probably already compromised the scene, so he didn't worry about fingerprints. Unlocking the driver side door, he paused. The scent of Adriana flowed out at him. It was strong, as if she sprayed herself with perfume inside the car. It reminded him of sage and fresh cotton, mystical and practical, though there seemed to be very little mystery about that woman.

He shined the light inside. Shit. The car was a mess of paper. The front seat had empty plastic bags and a crushed Kleenex box on the floor. The backseat was littered with receipts. He picked up a handful. Three fast food places, one organic grocery store, one gas station, one hardware store, two bank withdrawals, one restaurant and three sex store receipts. No surprise there. He picked up another handful. This one also included an oil change and a W-2.

Not exactly identity proof. Concerned, he sifted through a few more. She had check stubs, old bills and even a tax workbook CPAs often give clients to get ready for having their taxes done. If someone was in this car, they had access to her entire identity.

He shined the light over every inch, looking for any kind of clue. It wasn't as if he had a team of forensics experts at his beck and call, but at the moment he wished he did. Standing up, he shined the flashlight over the rest of the vehicle. There didn't appear to be any outside damage.

He strode around to the passenger seat and checked that window. There were no marks there. He tried the door and it remained locked. Returning to the driver's side, he sat in the seat and looked around. He could picture Adriana with the top down, her jet-black hair blowing in the wind as she sped down the highway, her smile wide or maybe she even laughed.

He envied her that. Despite her former career, she didn't appear disillusioned, just tough and she took life by the balls and squeezed every moment of joy from it she could. How did a person become like that?

He shook his head to refocus his thoughts. Opening the glove compartment, he found the registration and a couple of warnings for speeding. There was also a flashlight, a box of 9mm bullets, an array of condoms, a couple loose tampons and a pack of wet wipes. He was learning quite a bit about his coworker.

The passenger seat didn't have paper. It was piled with clothes. All looked brand new and sexy. Why wouldn't she have brought these down to her casita?

And why did he keep getting distracted? He needed to think of her as the victim. Would she even know if anything had been taken? This wasn't a good scenario. Stepping back out of the car, he was about to close the door when his flashlight glinted off something shiny under the driver seat. Crouching, he focused the light on the object.

Chapter Four

Hunter reached his hand beneath the seat and pulled out…a dog's tag? He palmed the small metal circle with a date on it and the word "rabies." It was from years ago. How long had it been since she cleaned her car out? Dropping the tag where it was, he rose and closed the door.

He kept the flashlight aimed at the floor and walked around the car. There was nothing else to see, so he wove his way out from between the staff cars. The rest, about fifteen, were all guests at the resort right now. With people leaving and coming all day, any possible evidence leading to who had broken into Adriana's car was probably gone, but he looked anyway.

He examined the cars, the floor, the walls, the desert outside the concrete slab that served as the floor of the three-sided garage. Old instincts from his first tour reawakened, giving him an energy he'd thought long dead.

When he finished scouring the immediate vicinity, he walked around the outside of the building, less to find clues than to walk off some of the buzz zipping through his brain. Now he wanted to talk to Adriana. Someone didn't break into a car for no reason. They needed to figure out why.

Once he'd completed his perimeter, he strode to the narrow canyon edge. From the top, he could see the whole resort, especially with the moon being as bright as it was. There was still one casita with lights on, number four. As he stared at it, a figure walked away and headed up the path to the main building.

It was Mac. Had she flashed and he'd missed it, so engrossed in his investigation? He jogged down the path, keeping his eye on her until he was too far below to see. She hadn't appeared to be in a hurry. It was important to back each other up.

By the time he made it to the fork in the dirt path, Mac was exiting the building. He strode toward her. "Mac."

She noticed him then and walked toward him. There was no saunter in her walk like Adriana. She was all business. "Did you find anything?"

"Yes. Any problems here? I saw you talking with the guests at casita number four."

"That was weird." She motioned with her thumb over her shoulder. "The foursome you talked about. They wanted to know if I knew where Adriana was. They said they'd invited her down but she hadn't arrived yet."

Hunter glanced toward the lit casita. "I guess she decided to stay home. What did you tell them?"

"I told them she'd probably gone to bed. They didn't like that answer."

"What do you mean?" His guard was on alert immediately.

Mac shrugged. "Just that the blonde started whining and her husband looked a bit insulted. I didn't realize Adriana was so important to the guests."

Shit, now he was getting ahead of himself. "I think only with those who are swingers or into other lifestyles. I doubt the nudist couples expect her to be visiting them at night."

"So what did you find up there?" Mac looked past him to where the garage sat.

"Let's walk." He headed them back toward the stables. "Someone broke into Adriana's car but didn't do any damage to it."

"Was anything taken?"

His lip twitched. "Hard to tell. I'll have to check with her tomorrow."

"Do you have any idea when it was broken into?" Her voice sounded more tense than usual.

"No."

As they crossed the fork between the two plateaus, he couldn't stop thinking about why someone would want to break into Adriana's car. The problem was, he knew nothing about her. Actually, he knew something. She was a former prostitute who came to work as a bartender at Poker Flat when Kendra asked her. He'd been told that by the boss herself.

He also knew Adriana loved sex and lots of kink. She was too exotic and sensual, and had an attitude that left no one in doubt about what she thought.

And she had nightmares.

Or it could have just been that one time because of the Dom. She'd shrugged off the experience, but she'd definitely been rattled by it.

"Hunter." Mac halted. "Do you think someone is stalking Adriana?"

"Don't know. She hasn't mentioned anything else unusual

happening. I probably won't have any theories until I talk with her, which will have to wait until she gets off work tomorrow."

"Okay. Keep me updated. I better get back to my rounds. A lot more happens out here in the middle of the desert than I ever expected." Mac shook her head before striding off toward the barn.

His gut told him she preferred watching over the horses and property as opposed to the guests. He didn't care which part of the resort he patrolled. His riding days were over, so if she wanted to guard the animals, it was fine with him.

Since Mac had already walked by the guest lodgings and main building, he headed for the staff casitas. Part of him wanted Adriana to have a light on so he could ask her some questions.

As he walked behind her casita, his wish was granted…sort of. There was a light on next to the couch where she lay sleeping on her side, a small brightly colored blanket pulled over her against the chill. She'd never even made it to the bedroom.

He stepped onto the patio, careful to stay out of the light in case she woke up. In sleep she was exquisite, each feature delicately sculpted. The loud personality was quiet, showing off her exotic beauty. Her black silky hair made her look like a dark goddess resting peacefully.

That wasn't her. If she saw him standing there, her lips would lift in a sultry smile and she'd invite him in where he could drown his sorrow and anger in her body. The temptation to knock was too much.

He spun on his heel and strode away.

~~~~~

Adriana smiled at an older couple, careful to keep her gaze trained on the woman. If there was one thing that would threaten Kendra's nudist resort, it was staff suspected of sleeping with guests behind the spouses' backs. She always made sure she grinned at the female until she learned the lay of the land. Besides, she didn't do men old enough to be her father anymore.

The couple smiled in return and continued on to the pool as she opened the large glass door to the main building. Lacey was busy with another pair checking in, so she waved and headed back to see Kendra. She was anxious to find out if Hunter had looked into her car.

She knocked on the open door, catching Kendra in a deep scowl. "Hey, boss, what's wrong? You look like you just discovered the resort is built on an ancient burial ground."

"Andy called in sick and the health inspector from the food and beverage department is up at the garage waiting, but I told Selma I'd give her a fifteen-minute warning, which you know means getting her to calm down so we don't get closed down because of her swearing. And of course our lunch rush started early today with the warm weather."

Adriana grinned. "No problem. I'm great at causing delays with men. Let me go meet the health inspector while you get Selma ready. I can open the bar when I get back. I'll just unlock the lower cabinets in case anyone needs alcohol with their lunch. Rachel can get it."

Kendra looked at her a moment. "That could work, though what I'll do with Andy gone all day, I don't know. Lacey says we have seven more check-outs and six check-ins."

"I'm thinking once the inspector is gone, you'll be free and once the lunch rush is done, Rachel will be free, so I can fill in in between and I'm sure we can get through the next couple hours. Where's Wade?"

Kendra rolled her eyes. "He's at the dentist. Not sure when he's going to come back."

"Finally getting that sore tooth checked out?"

Kendra stood and headed for the door. "Yeah. You'd think he was going in for major surgery. For a man who's ridden a bucking bronco, he can be a wuss sometimes."

Adriana followed Kendra out into the lobby. "I'll head up."

Kendra nodded but was already talking to Lacey.

Her boss would never say anything, but in conferring with Lacey, Adriana had figured out the vandalism last summer and the fire in October had seriously cut into the financial plan of the resort. They were supposed to have had more help by now. She sincerely hoped this busy season would be the boost Kendra needed to get over the hump.

After commandeering a golf cart, she drove down the path, across the wooden bridge and up the other side of the canyon in record time.

She'd worn an off-the-shoulder white blouse, her tan stretch gaucho pants and her brown cowboy boots today. Her straw cowboy hat completed the look. Her hair was already pulled back in a neat ponytail, so hopefully the inspector wouldn't get a bad impression.

It would be an interesting afternoon with them all juggling each other's jobs. Wade and Kendra usually filled in for sick employees, so she understood her boss' stress. Besides, who better to handle a male inspector than herself?

In no time, she'd flirted and engaged the older man, who seemed to be pretty curious about the resort anyway. She wouldn't be surprised if he showed up as a guest one day. They had lots of important people stay at Poker Flat because it was hidden away and the only photos allowed were those taken with permission. From what Lacey said, that was typical for nudist resorts.

After dropping off the inspector, she took over the bar. The stress was kind of fun, keeping her on her toes as she made drinks, flirted with guests and drove up to the garage a couple times. By late afternoon, everything had calmed down. Wade had returned, the inspector was gone, very impressed with Selma's kitchen, and she only had a few people at the outdoor bar.

"Adriana, how about another p-pina colada?" Patti, the swinger from the night before, stepped up to the bar.

"Of course. Anything else?"

"Can I get a kiss with that?"

She laughed. Generally she didn't do more than flirt while on shift, but since most of the guests were out at the pool and the only ones at the bar were the swingers, she just might.

"Here you go, Patti." She plunked down the cold, icy drink with a pineapple garnish.

Patti pouted as she took a sip. "And what about my k-kiss?"

"It will cost extra." She winked.

The slightly inebriated woman practically purred. "I'm willing to p-pay."

Adriana leaned over the bar, wrapped her hand around Patti's neck and kissed her. She slipped her tongue between the woman's lips and tasted the cold, sweet, creamy citrus of the drink. With a quick sweep of her tongue, she dominated the woman's mouth then quickly exited. The lack of turn-on concerned her.

Patti grinned. "Now I'm addicted."

Her husband pulled her against him. "And I'm jealous. My turn?" He wiggled his brow.

Adriana laughed to cover up her unease. "Not a chance. Save it for after dark. I'm on the clock."

"Adriana."

The hard tone of the voice had her turning. Wade stood at the entrance to the bar, frowning. The kiss wasn't *that* bad.

Wiping her hands on the bar towel, she turned away from her customers and walked over. "What's up?"

"Kendra wants to talk to you. I'll watch the bar."

That didn't sound good. "Okay." She lifted the bar top by Wade and slid out while he moved in. Either she'd screwed up something with the inspector or Kendra had a big problem.

Adriana picked up her pace as she headed into the main building. Out of habit, she glanced at the indoor bar. It was neatly buttoned up. If she'd screwed up, she'd fix it. She loved Poker Flat and respected Kendra. Hell, she'd been partly responsible for Wade and Kendra getting together. If there was anything she could do to help, she would.

She waved to Lacey who was helping a few guests, but Lacey's look told her things were not good. Damn.

She'd taken Kendra up on her offer to work at the resort because she was bored at the bordello. It certainly hadn't been a pay raise. But it hadn't taken her long to enjoy the unique vibe Kendra had created. All the staff were misfits and Adriana felt at home. There was no judgment, which was a good thing because she was not ashamed of her bordello days. She'd been damn good.

Now she was a damn good bartender and for the first time in her life, she felt like she had a real home, family, community that fit her perfectly.

She reached Kendra's closed door and knocked.

"Come in."

Opening it, she found her boss at her small round table off to the side with a couple of guests. She recognized them from the day before. She'd served them drinks at happy hour. "You needed me."

Kendra nodded. "Yes. The Blanchettes have come to me with a complaint I'm hoping you can shed some light on."

"Did I screw up on your drinks yesterday?" Her mind whizzed back. One high-end gin with tonic and a margarita, no ice.

Mrs. Blanchette flushed. "Hardly. Why did you call my husband this afternoon?"

"Huh? I didn't call him." She looked at Kendra. Did the man have a lady on the side and decide to blame it on her? She wasn't having any of that. "I've been running around like a crazy person between the golf cart rides, tending bar and the inspector."

The wife in her early forties glared at her. "That doesn't mean you couldn't make a phone call. Were you trying to get him to come out and meet you late at night while I was asleep?"

The husband touched his wife on the arm, probably hoping to calm her but it had the opposite effect. She whisked her arm away and stood to face Adriana.

The woman looked at her like she was the scum of the earth. "Just because you can't hold on to a man of your own, doesn't give you the right to come after someone else's."

What the fuck? "Listen, lady, I have no f—"

"Mrs. Blanchette, what made you think it was Adriana who called your husband?" Kendra's voice sounded pretty reasonable to her.

"You mean besides the fact she throws herself at every male guest here?"

The fucking bitch. She did no such thing. She was ultra-careful of that and was about to say so, but Kendra gave her the look that said to keep her mouth shut.

"When I asked who was calling, she chuckled and said it was Adriana." The woman nodded as if that sealed the deal.

Kendra didn't show any expression, which just added to Adriana's frustration. This was bullshit. It reminded her of eighth grade when the popular girls tried to pin crap on her because she was so much prettier than they were. Half the time it worked, but she was an adult now and she'd be damned if she'd let anyone accuse her of something she didn't do.

"Adriana, you can wait for me in the office." Kendra lifted an eyebrow, which made it clear she expected to be obeyed.

She bristled. "Gladly. But just so you know, if I were to go behind the back of a spouse, male or female, I certainly wouldn't tell the spouse my name. I'm not *that* stupid."

She ignored the gasp of the wife and stormed out of Kendra's office, too angry to watch where she was going. She'd made it to the lobby, almost bumping into a guest before she recognized where she was. "Damn." Turning back, she strode into the office behind the reception desk and flopped down in a chair at the table.

She'd probably just made Kendra's job all that much worse, but she'd be damned if she'd be accused of sleeping with a husband behind a wife's back. Her normal mode of operation was to do both, not one.

Did she have sex with guests when invited? Yes. Was she into different kinds of kink? Yes. But she damn well never went behind anyone's back and never let it interfere with her job.

Her gut tightened like she'd been punched. She'd *never* do anything to jeopardize Poker Flat.

Lacey poked her head in, her lavender-checked blouse making her look like an innocent cowgirl. "Hey, are you okay?"

The last thing Adriana needed was sympathy. "I'm fine. That bitch in there is the one with the fucking problem."

"Shhh." Lacey looked anxiously at the closed door. "I know. I was flabbergasted when they came to the desk. I ushered them back to Kendra right away. I didn't want anyone else hearing their accusations."

She stared hard at her friend. "Do you believe her?"

"Of course not." Lacey took the chair next to her. "You don't hide anything. Even if you wanted her husband, you would have just come out and propositioned them. That's just who you are."

Her stomach loosened a little at Lacey's words. "But do you think Kendra will believe me?"

Lacey looked away. "Probably, but she's got a bigger issue than believing you. If the Blanchettes go on the forums and start slamming this place because of what they think happened, we won't recover. The nudist community is tight."

"Motherfucker." So if Kendra couldn't convince the couple she was innocent, she'd be fired in order to keep the resort open. That sucked.

Lacey grasped her shoulder. "Don't worry. We'll figure this out."

"And if we don't, I guess I'll just have to leave." She shrugged. She'd been dealt worse blows in life. But the possibility still had her eyes smarting.

"No!" Lacey leaned forward and hugged her.

Freakin-a, she couldn't handle a Lacey hug right now. She wanted it too much. She disentangled herself from her friend. "Give a girl some room to breathe. Don't you have work to do or something?"

Lacey's eyes widened and she leaned back to check the front desk. She faced Adriana again. "Nope."

Great. "Did I tell you we need two bags of limes, a case of swizzle sticks and do you think you can order me some new bar towels? A few of them are getting pretty ratty-looking."

Lacey frowned. "No, you didn't tell me that. I just sent the order out. Let me see if I can add to it." Lacey stood in a flurry of white skirt and breezed through the door to the reception desk.

That worked like a charm. Now if she could just distract herself as easily as she distracted Lacey, she'd be in good shape. She should be out there tending bar, not sitting in a back room like she was in some kind of time out. If Kendra didn't come back in within the next five minutes, she was going back to work.

People's voices in the hallway caught her attention. She stood and moved closer to the door. From the tone, it sounded like Kendra had soothed the ruffled feathers of the guests. Good.

She walked back to the table and sat. What she'd like to know is why they were ruffled in the first place. Maybe the husband was fooling around with another woman and she used a staff name to deflect suspicion.

Hmm, that had to be it.

The door to the staff room opened and Kendra walked in.

"So, what's the real story?"

Her boss shook her head. "It's not good."

"What?" She stood. "I didn't do it." Her heart had gone into overdrive and she fisted her hands on her hips as she glared at Kendra.

"I know that." Kendra waved her aside, like that wasn't important. But it was to her.

"Sit. We need to talk."

"I don't want to sit or talk. I need to get back out to the bar."

Kendra was unmoved. Instead, she sat in the chair recently vacated by Lacey. "You can't go out to the bar. You are on vacation for a week."

"What? No, I'm not. You don't have enough staff for that."

"Yes, you are because if you go out there within the next week, the Blanchettes will post about your indiscretion in all the forums."

"Wait. *My* indiscretion? I didn't fucking do anything." Why was it that no one would listen to her? It was like she was invisible.

Kendra sighed. "*I* know that. *You* know that. Heck, the whole staff, once they hear of this event, will know you didn't do it. But the fact is, someone did call Mrs. Blanchette and they used your name. That is the only proof the Blanchettes, who don't know diddly about you, need."

Fuck. She paced to the other side of the room, one hand on her hip. "So why the forced vacation?"

"They agreed not to mention the event publically, if I put you on probation." Kendra held up her hand. "Wait. Hear me out. I told them I would do one better and force you to take a week off with no pay so you could think about your actions."

She fisted her hands, trying desperately not to hit anything. The urge to break something was strong.

"I also gave them three more nights for free. My hope is that while you are on 'vacation' whoever called Mr. Blanchette will call again, making it obvious it can't be you."

"Um, what does my being on vacation have to do with a call? People can call from anywhere."

Kendra suddenly found her jean-clad thigh fascinating and appeared to pick at a speck of whatever.

She didn't like it. "What aren't you telling me?"

"I told them I would confiscate your phone."

"Fuckin-a. I'm not a teenager who slipped out of her room at night and used Daddy's car. You're forgetting I didn't do anything wrong here."

Kendra's poker face fell and she sighed. "I know. I'm just trying to save Poker Flat and keep you on staff at the same time. Maybe that's not possible."

Dread at the prospect of Poker Flat closing or having to leave had the steam in her veins cooling. It infuriated her that someone had used her as their cover, but the last thing she wanted was to be the downfall of the resort. "Fine. But for the record, this blows."

At the relief in Kendra's face, her gut told her she'd done the right thing, but it still sucked…and it hurt.

Hunter strode toward the bar, his first step once starting his shift. He wanted to talk to Adriana and find out if she would be able to determine if anything was missing in her car. The mystery of the break-in had him anxious to get to work.

It was still early, the Arizona sky splashing a few purples

and reds across the Sonoran Desert. The inside lights of the main building were just discernable through the tinted glass windows.

He heard laughter in the bar area and quickened his step. As he turned the corner, he slowed. Kendra was tending bar. As far as he knew, she only filled in when employees were sick. Did Adriana's whip cuts become infected? He should have insisted on checking them the other night.

Despite his hatred for alcohol, he stepped up to the bar and waited for Kendra to finish with a guest. It was the same foursome from the other night. The tiny blonde woman teetered a bit as she took her wineglass with her, her husband keeping her from a serious face plant.

Hunter ground his teeth as a familiar burn started in the pit of his stomach.

"Do you need something, Hunter?"

He snapped his gaze away from the inebriated guest. "Is Adriana okay?"

Kendra sighed and that in itself sent sirens going off in his head.

"She's pretty upset." She leaned in and kept her voice low. "I had to put her on mandatory vacation."

He stared at her. "What exactly is that and why?"

Kendra glanced toward a couple walking up the path toward the bar. "I'll have to tell you later." In an instant, she was chatting with the two people.

But as Hunter watched, he could see the stiffness behind Kendra's smile and she leaned onto one hip, something he'd noticed she did when she was not comfortable.

He moved his gaze toward the guests. They ordered drinks

and waited, but they didn't chat or even look at each other. When he'd seen them a couple days ago they acted like two twenty year olds instead of a couple married for twenty years. Probably an argument.

He stepped away from the bar and strode back the way he'd come. The guest casitas could wait. He wanted to know what the hell was going on with Adriana.

It didn't take him long to reach her casita and without hesitation, he knocked on the door.

"I'm coming. Please don't leave. This solitary confinement is for the fucking birds." A crash sounded inside and he had to tap down his instinct to bust in the door. It wasn't as if she was some kind of criminal, but if she was scrambling to hide a guest, Kendra would be pissed.

More shuffling sounds came from inside. "Just had to throw something on."

He almost grinned at that. Since when?

Finally, the door was yanked open.

"Oh my God. Thank you." Adriana jumped onto him, her legs wrapping around his waist as her arms encircled his neck.

Before he could figure out what she was grateful for, she'd pressed her lips against his and thrust her tongue into his mouth.

Every nerve in his body ignited and he grasped her against him. He captured her tongue with his own and swept through her mouth, tasting a bite of lemon and inhaling her fresh sage scent.

Adriana pulled back and looked at him with full-on lust. "Hi."

CHAPTER FIVE

Every part of his body wanted to back Adriana against the outside wall and take her right there. He swallowed and forced himself to focus. "Something's wrong."

She frowned before dropping her legs to stand, but she didn't back away. "You can say that again."

He didn't move. He couldn't. If he did, he'd be ripping her clothes off like an animal. He focused on his breathing, in and out, keeping his in-take even with his out-take while ignoring his hard cock.

"Some stupid bitch accused me of sleeping with her husband." She let go of his neck and placed her hand on her hip. "As if I was that desperate." She raised her other hand and snapped her fingers. "I can have my pick of those who are free to indulge. Why would I go behind some wife's back to sleep with her husband?"

"For the challenge?" He purposefully incited her. Something in his masculine brain wanted to see her out of control. Maybe to retaliate for making him almost lose his own.

Her eyes turned to slits before she wrinkled her nose and

spat on the ground. Then she thrust her chin up at him. "I have standards. I'm not a home wrecker. I don't submit. I don't ever put Poker Flat at risk. You got that?" She rose on her toes to get in his face.

He barely kept his lips from quirking up. "Got it."

She scowled at him a moment longer before she stepped back. "I'm under house arrest."

"What?" That didn't make sense.

She threw her hands up. "I might as well be. I'm not allowed to go back to work for a week."

"Kendra believed the guest?" He found that difficult to swallow. He didn't know his boss very well, but from what he knew, she was very protective of her staff.

Adriana's face softened. "No, she didn't, but she had to do something or this couple could say nasty things about the resort, which would keep anyone from ever coming here again."

He doubted one disgruntled customer could do that much damage, but he was no expert on the nudist community. Shit, he hadn't even known there was such a community until his old high school buddy, Dale, asked him to apply at Poker Flat.

"And as if being off work for a week for something I didn't do wasn't punishment enough, Kendra confiscated my phone. The bitch claimed I called her husband. All you have to do is look at my outgoing calls and they could easily see I didn't call, but Kendra had to pacify the customer." Adriana crossed her arms over her ample chest. "I haven't talked to anyone since this afternoon." She pouted in an effort to enlist sympathy, but her full lips were far too sexy to make that work.

To him it was more of an invitation to take off her clothes and he was on duty. If there was one thing therapy had done for him, it was teach him how to refocus. "Your car was broken into."

Adriana's eyes widened before she let out a yell. "Yes! I knew it."

Her whole body relaxed, which had his lips itching to smile. Most women would be devastated. "Do you think you could tell if anything was taken?"

She gave him a seductive look. "You bet I can. I know every item that's in that car. It's my organized mess. It helps to keep my casita clean. Can't stand clutter."

He raised an eyebrow in disbelief. "What about the rabies tag?"

Her face softened, her brows drawing together. "That was Lady's. I keep it under the driver's seat."

The expression was so unusual on her that he had to ask. "Lady?"

She looked away. "She was my dog. A sweet little terrier who didn't mind wearing a pink bow once in a while. A client had given her to me as partial payment. I didn't want her at first, but the silly thing seemed to live for my every glance. It was the oddest relationship, but we got along fine."

He had to ask. "What happened to her?"

Adriana, lost in her memories, appeared startled, but she covered it up with a shrug. "She died. They only live so long."

Her reaction was forced indifference. She'd loved that dog. He didn't say anything, processing this surprising information. She was far more complicated than she first appeared. He'd bet most people didn't realize exactly how complicated or how intelligent the woman was.

Eventually, she put her hand on her hip and caught his gaze. "So now that we know my car was broken into, what do we do?"

"That depends, was anything taken?"

"No." She scrunched her nose. "I can't believe they went to the trouble of breaking into my car and didn't take anything. Not a single receipt was missing. Even my bullets were still in the glove compartment."

He wanted to ask more about that, but as it wasn't relevant to the issue at hand, he moved on. "That could be because someone was interrupted before they could take something or because they just wanted to see if they could get in so they could come back another time when they thought it would be safe to steal it."

"I would be devastated if that car was stolen. It means a hell of a lot more to me than just a vehicle for driving around. That's a symbol."

Before he could clamp his mouth shut, he'd opened it. "Symbol of what?"

"My independence from my past."

"You mean from the bordello? I had the distinct impression you enjoyed that job."

She winked at him. "You bet I did. Though now that I'm here, I'm glad that part of my life is over. No, my car is older than that. I bought it a year after I started at Mrs. B's. I bought it outright. Cash."

Adriana's eyes sparkled in the dim light of her outside light, her energy reaching across the feet that separated them to make him feel her thrill.

"Once I'd done that, I knew I could leave anytime I wanted. It also symbolized my ability to have and do whatever I wanted in life. That's why it was so easy to leave when Kendra offered me the job. I didn't owe Mrs. B anything."

"Did she try to force you to stay?"

Adriana laughed. "No, nothing like that. She more or less begged and cajoled me to stay because after ten years I was her most profitable girl." She grinned in pure feminine satisfaction. "But it was time to move on."

He found himself nodding, as if he could possibly understand what it was like to be a prostitute who left a bordello. He stopped. It had to be her refreshing honesty. Every emotion or thought appeared on her face and in her words. Nothing was held back. He liked that.

A memory of his wife pretending to like the rodeo because he did came unbidden to his mind. She'd loved him so much, she'd have done anything he liked. It had taken him awhile to finally realize that. Too long. He hadn't appreciated what he had.

"Would you like to come in? I could sure use the company. I promise not to attack you again…unless you want me to." Adriana winked.

"I'm on patrol." The words came out in a rush. "Thanks anyway." He gave her a curt nod and strode off toward the next staff casita to make sure everything was okay, and not because he was running away.

Adriana walked back into her casita. That man was a puzzle and she so wanted to put him together and find out what the answer was.

She turned off the television, the noise of having it on all day finally getting to her. Picking up her laptop, she flopped onto her love seat. She clicked it on and pulled up a game. Not working was driving her crazy. After killing a few monsters and getting into the secret passageway, she paused the screen.

If she had to be bored, the least she could do is have a drink with her boredom. After taking down a wineglass, she uncorked a new bottle of red wine and poured. It felt odd drinking alone. Whatever. It wasn't like she had a choice.

Pushing the cork back into the bottle, she put it on the counter and walked back to her couch. She glanced outside, noticing the light shining from her living room onto her patio, just like it did with the guest casitas. Would Hunter come by again tonight to make sure all was safe?

Yes. He would.

Suddenly, the distraction of the game wasn't enough. She could masturbate in the living room and watch for the telltale black cowboy boots to show up. Just the image of that had her body sensitized. But as she let the fantasy play out in her mind, it wasn't as exciting as it used to be.

Because now she wanted him. She'd felt the hard muscle of his body when she'd jumped onto him. It could have been anyone at her door, but riding his waist had sparked fireworks inside her. He hadn't even taken a step back as she threw herself into his arms. The man was a hunk.

He did want her. At least his kiss said he did. Of course he did. She was hot. And how long had it been since he'd been with a woman? Her gut told her not since before he arrived at Poker Flat last October.

Mackenzie was an amazon and just as hard bodied. It was doubtful those two had sex. They were more like comrades in arms. She grinned at the thought.

Why not? She and Hunter were consenting adults. It's not like she wanted a relationship. Those were way too sticky. As the idea grew, the more convinced she was that it was a perfect ending to a boring day.

Jumping up, she sauntered into her room. Now what to wear? Nothing frilly for him. She prided herself on reading men's likes. No, Hunter would like casual sexy, which fit her perfectly.

Pulling off her yoga pants, she wiggled into a pair of cut off, denim shorts, nothing underneath. Something simple for a top. A red, no-sleeve button-down that tied beneath her breasts would work. She looked at herself in her full-length, three-way mirror. One more thing.

Grabbing up a clip, she twisted her long hair up like she did when bartending and stuck the clip in it. Slightly messy. Perfect. She gave herself a sultry smile.

Oh yeah, she would be getting some tonight.

She pulled on a pair of short socks and her cowboy boots that made her legs look awesome. Jumping up from her bed, she grabbed her lock pick from her jewelry box. She paused. Last time he'd been pretty pissed she was in his casita. But what was she supposed to do, sit in a chair outside?

No way, but she could prepare him. Turning the light off in her bedroom, she moved back into the living room to her desk against the far wall. She pulled out a piece of scrap paper with an expired coupon for twenty-five percent off a vibrating anal wand and with a red marker she drew the female symbol intersecting with the male symbol. That should give him a hint.

She laughed, thrilled with her plan of action. Now all she needed to do was wait until the early hours of the morning. She didn't know much about Hunter, but he was definitely a cowboy, which meant he wouldn't leave his job one minute before it was done. It hadn't taken long to figure that out.

Maybe she could make him that breakfast she'd suggested the other morning.

Adriana busied herself with packing up breakfast ingredients, snacks, sex toys and condoms in between playing games and fantasizing. When two o'clock finally rolled around, she grabbed her basket of goodies and turned out the lights.

After locking her casita, she walked past two others before coming to Hunter's. With expert finesse, she unlocked his door and stuck the sign on the outside before closing the door and relocking it. Once she'd put all the cold stuff in the fridge, she sat on his couch to wait.

Just a few more hours and he would be coming home. Her imagination started to go wild.

Hunter filled in Mac on what had happened with Adriana. They also took turns patrolling the garage. After what Adriana had told him about her car, he didn't want anything else to happen to it.

The woman intrigued him. She was very honest in her immediate reactions, but there was another layer to her he hadn't expected. He probably should have. Everyone had a past.

He grunted as his own rose up to choke him. Forcing it away from his thoughts, he strode to his casita. The sun had yet to come up, the sky just barely starting to lighten. It wasn't much past five, but Selma had already opened the kitchen and Jorge was feeding the horses.

Kendra had closed the bar by one, which had left only one

casita active for most of the night. When the foursome saw him, they'd asked him to ask Adriana to come down. He should have passed along the message, but he hadn't. He didn't know why, but it was probably better. Adriana had enough crap to handle between her car and the angry guest.

As he approached his home, a paper fluttered against the door. Curious, he pulled out his flashlight since the predawn light had yet to make it to that side of his casita. He stared at the symbols.

"Adriana." His cock jerked. "Shit." She'd picked his lock again.

He didn't move to open the door. She was inside and he was off work. Was there any reason not to take what she offered?

If it had been anyone else, the answer would have been not a chance, but Adriana was different. Sex was given freely and often, no strings attached. That's the part that was unusual. Sex meant something to women. To Adriana, it meant pleasure and no more.

His cock hardened. It knew sex with her would be good. It was a basic animal need, that's all.

Even as the possibility enticed his body, Julie clung hard to his heart.

Everything feminine, sweet, innocent and loyal was embodied in his late wife. She would have made an amazing mother. They were supposed to grow old together and teach their grandchildren how to ride.

Doubt crept through his dreams of what should have been. Could they have found that peace after he came home the second time?

He stood three feet from his door and stared at the drawing fluttering slightly as the temperature started to change and sent small disturbances through the air. It had been hard returning after the first tour. It had taken him almost six months to readjust to being around Julie after seeing the horrors that were the reality on the other side of the globe.

This tour had been far worse. If she hadn't been in the accident, could they have had the future they'd dreamed of, or had he already killed it and didn't know it? Was her accident and subsequent death a blessing in disguise?

"No." He grabbed the paper and ripped it down. Julie deserved to live and in death continued to be an angel.

Unlocking his door, he strode in, ready to boot Adriana out. What right did she have to come into his space? Into his head?

He didn't turn on the light as he silently let himself in. Instead, he used his flashlight. Maybe if he scared her, she'd get the message.

He assumed she'd be in his bedroom and headed that way when he caught sight of her on the couch. She was asleep, curled up to fit on the love seat.

He moved the light to reflect off the title floor. Even in sleep the woman looked sexy, as if she beckoned him to enjoy her charms.

Had she always had this aggressive sexual demeanor? What would that have been like when she was a teenager? Did men approach her? Even as his gut answered yes, his mind rebelled at what might have occurred. Were all women jealous of her like the guest wife? How did she make female friends? Or did she?

Better yet, why should he care? Fuck.

He turned off the flashlight and strode into his room. He shouldn't be thinking of Adriana and what her life was like. The woman wanted sex and a lot of it and right now she happened to want him.

She had a past. Who didn't, but she was just a coworker. Nothing more.

Stripping, he threw his clothes on the bench at the end of his bed and lay down. He needed to stop thinking of having sex with her. It wasn't going to happen. He was at Poker Flat to protect the staff, not fuck them. He wasn't going to start screwing up Adriana's life too.

Closing his eyes, he rolled onto his side, focused on the image of the last sunset and took deep, even breaths.

Eventually, he drifted off…and the dreams began.

"Sargent Hunter. Please come with me."

"But my wife will be waiting for me."

The corporal refused to meet his eyes.

They had to let him see Julie. It had been over a year since he'd been home, but his training wouldn't be denied and he followed the corporal away from the terminal exit and into an airline lounge.

"Major Swanson will be right out." The corporal disappeared.

He looked at his phone. Julie knew he'd arrived in Phoenix. She'd be anxiously watching every passenger from his plane, her eyes lighting when a uniform walked out of the A gates and into the main terminal only to be disappointed when it wasn't him.

Hunter glanced at the door he'd just come through. Whatever it was, the Army could wait. They knew where to find him. He stepped toward the exit when the door opened and a major he'd never met before walked in. He stood at attention and saluted.

"At ease, sergeant. I know you are anxious to see your wife, but she's not here. We have a car waiting to take you to Van Buren Memorial Hospital where she's receiving the best care possible."

"What? What are you talking about? I just talked to my wife

when I changed planes in Chicago. I think you have me mixed up with someone else."

The major studied him. "Your wife is Julie McKade, isn't she?"

His heart tripped, making it hard to breathe as a wave of fear froze his blood. "Yes."

The major put his hand on his shoulder. "I'm sorry, son." His mind refused to listen. "There was an accident...a tractor trailer... drunk driver...coma..." The words blurred as pain ricocheted through him.

"No." He shook his head. "No. No. No!" he lashed out, fighting off the major and others as they tried to restrain him. No. Not Julie, his life, his love, his reason for making it home.

The scent of sage and linen filled his nostrils, softening the edges of his dream. The harsh lines of glass and steel rounded into saguaro cacti and mesquite trees. Warmth, not cold, recycled air, permeated his back and the image of an old withered male face was replaced with laughing brown eyes and enticing lips. Silky soft hair brushed against his shoulder, soothing the tension in his muscles.

Gentle arms wrapped around him, held him tight. He sank into the peace that filled his senses, luxuriating in it like the warm therapy tub he'd used to recover in, letting it seep into every part of his being. He greedily took it in, his soul thirsty for comfort and relief.

Adriana held on to Hunter until his breathing returned to normal and the steel-hard tension of his body finally relaxed. Then she continued to hold him, still baffled by her own actions.

When his yell woke her, she was disoriented, having forgotten where she was for a moment. At first her ego kicked her hard for being somewhere she wasn't wanted, just before she started scolding herself for falling asleep. But when another yell and an agonized groan came from Hunter's bedroom, she was compelled to check on him.

Whatever the dream was about, it was a bad one. A faded memory from her childhood pushed its way past her blockade, forcing her to acknowledge a time when her beautiful but spineless mother had eased her fear by cocooning her in bed.

Hoping it would help, she crawled onto Hunter's bed, still clothed, of all things, and held on to him, pressing herself against his back, her arm wrapped around his waist. He started to calm immediately, which made her feel inordinately pleased with herself.

Damn, she'd never been in bed with a man this long and remained fully clothed. Though she'd usually view that as a failure on her part, she didn't feel that way at all. She felt good that she'd been able to help him calm down. Maybe she'd scared the nightmare away.

She liked that idea. Adriana. Nightmare Slayer. She silently chuckled. Looked like she had another talent she could add to her list.

Hunter's breathing grew deep, as if he hadn't truly slept in months. Maybe sleeping during the day didn't agree with him. She glanced toward the window where the blinds were closed tight. Still, she could see the sun had risen over the high ground and light would soon be beating down on the resort within the old ravine.

She was loath to leave his side. She liked holding him. There was more male in his body than in any three she'd slept with since coming to Poker Flat. She'd *never* comforted a man before. She'd given out her fair share of hugs at Mrs. B's, especially to Lynzie. That poor girl had wanted a child so bad and every time she didn't conceive, it was another bout of tears.

But a man? Men didn't need comfort. They just bulldozed their way through life like they pounded themselves between her legs. Even her father, while lying in a puddle of blood, still managed to shoot off his gun, refusing to admit he was dying.

She blinked at the memory and shoved it aside. Hunter's past was slowly becoming an addiction and without any work to occupy her, she needed to figure it out or go crazy.

Slowly, she lifted her arm and forced herself to move away. She stood and stared at the naked man who had been her fantasy. His back was a mass of muscles with definition standing out even in their resting position. His hard white ass appeared sculpted from marble and the backs of his thighs held shadowed lines, emphasizing how taut they were.

But below his thighs his perfection ended. Scars were everywhere, as if he's been on the barrel end of a shotgun. The other place he had his fair share of scars was the back and top of his head. No wonder the man wore his hair so short and kept his cowboy hat on all the time. It looked like Picasso had etched a painting on his head. Another puzzle piece.

He lay on his left side, but his right arm had a few tattoos. She loved tattoos. Had one herself. One of Hunter's tattoos was a name. Beyond curious, she leaned on the bed and looked at it closer. It *was* a name.

Julie.

Hmm, ex-wife or girlfriend? He definitely hadn't had any woman with him at Poker Flat and since he lived in his casita, that meant he was single. She stood straight again. Perfect. That meant he was definitely for the taking.

But not now. As much as she wanted to ride him like a cowgirl should, his deep sleep, which she took complete credit for, wasn't something she wanted to disturb. Maybe this evening before he had to go to work.

Quietly, she left the room and headed for the door, still baffled that she was letting a hunky naked man sleep. She grabbed up her cowboy hat and stilled. Did he not want to have sex because she was asleep or because he wasn't interested?

She shook her head. What was she thinking? Of course he was interested. He was just being a cowboy. Too damn polite. Opening the front door, she looked back toward his room and blew him a kiss. "Later, cowboy." She closed the door quietly and turned.

Lacey stood there staring at her with wide eyes, a to-go package in her hands.

She put her hand out to stop her friend. "He's sleeping. Don't disturb him."

Lacey's brow furrowed. "I wasn't looking for Hunter. I was looking for you."

"You found me." She grinned. "Oh, is that for me? If it is, I love you and will forever." She strode toward Lacey, smelling the air as she moved closer.

Lacey glanced back at Hunter's casita, so Adriana took advantage of her distraction and took the package from her before heading for her own place.

"Adriana, wait."

"Uh-uh, this feels warm and smells like one of Selma's breakfast burritos. I'm not waiting for anyone."

Lacey caught up with her just as she unlocked her door.

"I hope this was meant for me because if this was yours, you're going to have to get another." Selma rarely allowed staff to take to-go boxes because she felt strongly that they should "break bread" together.

Lacey followed her inside. "No, that was for you. I was hoping to cheer you up, but it appears you are already pretty happy with yourself."

At the perturbed tone in her friend's voice, she paused halfway through opening the container on her kitchen counter. "What? Because I was at Hunter's? There's no policy saying staff can't have sex with each other."

Having put that to rest, she pulled a fork from the drawer and dug into the spicy egg concoction.

"It's not always about policy, Adriana. Sometimes it's about being sensitive to others."

She stilled, the food an inch from her mouth. "What do you mean, sensitive?"

Lacey dropped onto a stool across from her. "Like having a little compassion. Geeze, the man just lost his wife a little over a year ago. I doubt he's in any shape to have a relationship."

His wife died? She put down her fork, the food untouched. Multiple feelings swirled through her, none of them good. "Who said I wanted a relationship? You know me better than that."

"That's just the thing. I doubt the guy wants just sex. How must he feel?"

A knot formed in her stomach. "He's a man. If he lost his wife I'll bet some meaningless sex is just what he needs."

Lacey clasped her hands in front of her, a sure sign she was really bothered.

"Listen, hon, don't worry. I didn't have sex with Hunter. I just cuddled with him a bit, which helped him sleep."

Lacey's eyes grew wide. "Don't lie to me. I'm not stupid and you don't have to protect me. I thought you realized that last time we went lingerie shopping together."

She couldn't help her grin. It had been fun watching her sweet friend try on some wild lingerie, Lacey's one fetish, but the questions from Whisper, Lacey's friend, had Adriana laughing out loud even while relating the stories to guests weeks later.

"Lacey, I'm not lying to you. I'd never do that with you. The fact is, I went over to Hunter's to seduce him but fell asleep and believe it or not, he didn't wake me up." She didn't feel the need to tell Lacey about the nightmare he'd had. "When I woke, I cuddled with him for a while. But he was in such a deep sleep, I didn't have the heart to wake him."

Lacey studied her. "I'm sorry. It was just a little hard to believe."

"I know. I'm still shocked myself." She winked then dipped her fork into her breakfast again.

"I feel so bad for him." Lacey paused to watch her take her first mouthful and moan. "You know, I didn't care for him at first, but when Kendra hired him, I knew there must be a reason."

Lacey may not let her see Hunter's profile, but it appeared she was open to talking about him. "You mean in addition to the fact he does a damn good job and moves around this resort so quietly even the desert mice don't realize he's there?"

Lacey smiled. "Yeah, there is that."

She took another bite of her breakfast, trying to appear casual when her stomach was so tight, she questioned whether she should be eating at all. "So what's his story? I mean, everyone here is on their second chance."

Lacey clasped her hands. "I think for him it is more just being able to function in civilian life. He went back to the police department, but things didn't exactly work out. I think Dale tried to place him at a number of jobs, but as far as I know, this is the longest one he's been at."

She nodded as if she understood. Anything to keep Lacey talking.

"He has all kinds of medals from his service to our country, but to come home and find his wife was on life support must have been devastating."

Adriana felt the mouthful of egg she just swallowed stick halfway down to her stomach. Crap. He must have been a mess. He had to have really loved his wife to have her name tattooed on his arm.

Love was something she knew nothing about and stayed very far away from.

The problem was, the more she learned about him, the more she wanted to know. But she was about sex, keeping it nice and clean. Maybe that's why he didn't take her up on her offer. He didn't think he could have sex because she might want more.

"Adriana, what are you thinking?"

She shrugged. "I'm thinking maybe I can offer him exactly what he needs. A warm body to sink into and forget about his woes for a while. Just sex."

"I don't think he's wired that way." Lacey cocked her head, her look doubtful.

"Lacey, war changes people. All that blood and guts and killing." She shivered just from saying the word *blood* out loud. "He may need a little hot sex to escape his misery and his celibacy." She wiggled her brows.

Lacey moved off the stool. "You two are adults. You certainly don't need me looking over your shoulder."

"If—"

Lacey raised her hand. "No, I don't want to watch. Cole is all I need, thank you."

"And a little lingerie." She winked. "What are you wearing today?"

Lacey used to blush around her, but she'd become more comfortable with the teasing. "The open nipple bra and crotchless panties. I'll put the three-way clips on once I get home. Cole would kill me if I wore those to work."

Adriana laughed. "I'm so proud of you. Just wait until you do wear a toy or two to work. You won't be able to wait for Cole to strip."

Lacey shook her head even as she moved to the door. "Nope. Toys aren't my main thing, but some accessories now and then really heat things up for Cole."

"Honey, what do you expect? The man is a freakin' firefighter."

Lacey laughed and let herself out.

The casita became too quiet and Adriana turned on the television to add some noise. Lacey had spilled a lot more about Hunter than expected, but then again, the easiest way to get Lacey to talk was to get her concerned about someone.

Adriana snorted. That Lacey felt the need to protect Hunter, a veteran, a former police officer, from her was silly. Hunter could take care of himself and if she had her way, he'd take care of her too, no strings attached, unless of course there were nipple clips at the end.

Chapter Six

Hunter woke before the alarm. No surprise there, but something was wrong. The buzz next to his bed explained why he woke. Picking up his phone, he answered. "Hunter."

"I need you to come to my office right now." Kendra sounded furious. "We have a fucking security issue that could put this place under."

"Be there in two." He hung up and grabbed a clean pair of jeans. He felt strangely well-rested despite the fact the sun hadn't set yet.

In two minutes, he was dressed and headed out the door, a mint in his mouth and a gun tucked into his pants. He strode straight to Kendra's office, scanning the resort for trouble.

Maybe someone had stolen Adriana's car after all, or maybe many cars. He glanced up at the garage but didn't see any police lights, so he pulled the glass door of the main building open and headed for the employee hallway. Lacey was already gone and the front desk was left in muted lighting. Guests knew to call the service line and whoever had duty, usually Kendra or Wade, helped them out.

Kendra's office door was closed so he knocked before he opened it and walked in.

Kendra and Wade were staring at her computer screen.

Wade glanced up. "Hunter. Come look at this."

He stepped behind the desk and Wade moved over so he could see. On the screen was a picture of a man. His face was clear, but from the neck down it had been purposefully blurred. Still, he could make out it was an older man with a bit of belly lounging by the pool at the resort. "What am I looking at?"

"You are looking at Judge Landry. He spent the day here last weekend."

"Okay." He still wasn't sure how this was a security breach.

Kendra hit the back button on her computer and the picture shrunk to a thumbnail size and next to it was a price along with his name. Even as he looked, the price next to the picture rose.

It didn't take long to understand what was going on. "Someone is selling naked pictures of guests who would rather no one know they were here to the highest bidder."

Kendra's free hand curled into a fist as she worked the mouse with her other. "Not someone." She clicked on the amount and the payment screen came up. She moved the cursor to the name where the money was being sent.

Adriana Perez.

Hunter gritted his teeth to keep an immediate denial from escaping. His gut told him this was bullshit. "Do you think Adriana is selling pictures of guests on the internet?"

Kendra looked at him like he had two heads. "What do you think?"

He tamped down his need to defend her. He'd examine that

knee jerk reaction later. "The first thing we need to do is get that site down." He had no doubt the resort would go under if it stayed live and word spread, which it would.

His need to stop that from happening just proved how much he'd already come to consider the resort home. It wasn't much, but it was all he had. "I have a friend in…let's just say I know someone who can get this site shut down immediately. Let me make a call."

Kendra's relief was palpable. "Thank you."

He strode from the office and out the front door where the cell phone reception was best. He didn't believe for one minute that Adriana was selling pictures. Someone wanted to make her life miserable.

Within minutes he'd talked to his friend in intelligence. A friend he'd made when he saved the man's life on his first tour. Not only would he shut down the site, but do a little digging into who set it up and where they might be. Hunter reached for the door when Mac appeared.

"I just got the message we have a serious issue."

He opened the door for her. "Yeah, I'm hoping I took care of the immediate threat, but you better come in."

Once back in Kendra's office, he walked behind her again. "Mac, take a look at this. Kendra, don't change screens."

Mac stepped up next to him. "What the hell?"

Kendra nodded. "That was my reaction."

Hunter pointed to the top of the screen. "Take a screen shot. I want to examine this further, then refresh."

Kendra did as instructed and a sad face came up with the words "We are having temporary difficulties."

She snapped her head up to look at him. "So what does that mean? Will it come back up?"

"It means I have had the site shut down, but to those who were bidding, they will think they just need to wait for it to be fixed."

"But it won't go back up?"

He shook his head. "No, it won't." He stepped around to the front of the desk, the number of people behind it getting too crowded for him. "Where is Adriana?"

They all looked at him in surprise.

"You did call her to confront her about this, right?" He hated people going behind others' backs.

Wade recovered first. "We can't call her. Kendra has her cell phone."

"I'll go get her." He wanted to tell her and see her reaction first. His gut told him this was too coincidental. He didn't believe in coincidence and that belief had saved his life twice.

Kendra finally recovered and nodded. As he headed down the hall, he heard movement behind him. By the time he reached the front door, Mac had caught up.

She fell into step next to him. "You don't think Adriana did this."

"No. I don't. Do you?"

She shook her head. "I don't know her very well, but she doesn't strike me as the type to sneak around. She's just so…"

"Obvious?"

Mac grinned. "Yeah."

Hunter slowed his step. "Can you cover the whole resort for an hour or so? I want to get to the bottom of this as soon as possible."

"Sure. No problem. Let me know what you discover."

"I will." Hunter watched Mac head for the stable side of the resort. He liked that he could count on her if he needed to. Having a dependable comrade in arms was critical to survival…except this wasn't survival.

He made himself continue to Adriana's. Would he ever get out of military mode? Even if he did, the cop in him might never leave.

He hadn't even reached the casita before Adriana came out.

"Where were you? You were supposed to still be asleep. I went over to make you dinner and you were already gone."

He stopped in front of her, aware of her irritation at having her plans thwarted. He'd planned to tell her in her casita, but if his instinct was correct, outside might be better. "Kendra called me to come in early due to a serious security breach."

Adriana put her hand on her hip and scowled. "It had better be really serious to wake you up early. You were in a deep sleep when I left you. It's not right to call you in early."

Her pique over his inconvenience surprised him. "It was very serious. Someone has posted naked photos of important people who have visited the resort and is selling them online."

"What? They can't do that! The resort will crumble back to the dust it came from. Oh my God, Kendra has got to be beside herself. We have to do something." She started to walk past him as if she could fix everything immediately.

He wasn't surprised. He grabbed a hold of her arm. "Wait. There's more."

Her eyes widened in dread, and she grabbed his arm in return. "Tell me."

"The site shows you as the one selling them."

Adriana's eyes widened more even as her fingernails bit into his biceps. Her brows lowered before she opened her mouth. "Motherfucker!" She dropped his arm and stomped away but turned back to face him, her hand flying up in the air. "This is that fucking Dom's doing. He's getting back at me for *his* loss of control. He can't go to any nudist resorts, so he wants to get me fired."

Adriana took a second to take in more air. Her chest heaved with anger and her eyes were glittering dangerously. If it wasn't such a serious issue, he'd be unable to resist fucking her right there on the ground. Shit, the woman was a walking temptation.

She glared at him. "Kendra knows I'm not behind this, right?"

He didn't answer. He thought it might be the Dom as well, but Adriana could have other enemies. "Is there anyone else who may want to see you fired from this position, such as Mrs. B or an old client? What about other guests? The woman who accused you of sleeping with her husband?"

Adriana didn't answer. She'd noticed he hadn't answered her and even in the dying rays of the sun, he caught the flash of hurt in her eyes before she pulled herself together. "I think it's the Dom, but it could be someone else. I did refuse to date a guy from town that I had a one-night stand with. He wanted more and started pestering me, but he stopped a couple weeks ago. All the guests this week, except that Mrs. Blanchette, have seemed friendly."

At her mention of her one-night-stand, he tensed. He didn't like the idea that her former lovers might come looking for her. "What about unruly guests at the bar?"

She flipped her hair over her shoulder. "I've only had three in the last three months and the next mornings they didn't appear to hold a grudge that I had shut them off."

His mind raced with possibilities. "Did any of them leave before you saw them again?"

Adriana squinted for a few seconds then looked at him again. "No. All three were here the next morning."

That ruled that out. They probably wouldn't find any good clues until his buddy in intelligence traced the site origin. In the meantime, Adriana had the right to have her say in front of her boss. "I don't think we'll solve this tonight, but you need to tell Kendra what you know."

Adriana's hands flew up. "I don't know anything. That's the problem."

He nodded as he walked toward her. The urge to comfort rose hard, and he struggled to keep it at bay.

She looked into his eyes and her look of angry hopelessness was too much to ignore.

He pulled her face toward his and kissed her, hard. Instinct told him she wasn't one to appreciate soft. His instinct was right. She wrapped her arms around his neck and pushed her tongue into his mouth, wrestling with his own.

Her taste filled his senses, chocolate, fruit and a flavor all her own, even as her scent enveloped him. She was all woman, sexy, curvy, and full of life.

The heat between them rose fast. His hand found her ass and he pushed her pelvis against his hardening cock, letting her know he wanted her. He grasped the silky strands of black hair and forced her to angle her face, allowing him better access to her mouth.

It was sexual anticipation and it felt good, right, hot. His body came alive to another level of feeling and need flooded him. Lust, pure and simple, moved him to leave her full lips and suck her neck, nibbling at the intoxicating skin.

He wanted her, here. Now. He sucked at the hollow where her neck met her shoulder and her nails dug into his back. A heady moan vibrated through her throat and into his ear.

He sucked harder, like a man whose life depended on hanging on to the dusky skin beneath his lips.

Movement in his peripheral vision had him letting up. He looked past the pulse that called to his dark side. Mac's gaze met his for an instant before she continued her route by the staff casitas.

He could continue to feed the hunger inside, but his brain grappled with his lust and finally regained control. Carefully, he pulled Adriana upright and loosened his hold until she regained her own balance.

Stepping away, he looked her in the eye. "You need to talk to Kendra."

She took a deep breath and nodded. "I do." Stepping past him, she started for the main building.

He followed, ignoring the swing of her hips by keeping his gaze on the path ahead of her. He took deep breaths like they'd taught him, but his calm was only surface deep. It felt like he'd poked a hole in the dam holding his desire at bay and now the only thing keeping back the flood waters was one finger that itched to be free.

She didn't wait for him to open the door at the main building, but instead marched straight down to Kendra's office. Nor did she stop to knock before opening the door.

"You think I did that?" She pointed to the computer Kendra sat in front of.

Hunter felt a strange pride in Adriana for taking the offensive. He leaned against the doorframe to see how it played out.

Their boss stood. "What am I supposed to think? Your name is listed as the one taking in the money."

Adriana strode straight up to the desk and put both hands on her hips. "Since when do I need fucking money?" She lifted a hand and pointed at Kendra. "And since when did you start doubting me?"

Kendra's face changed to poker mode, but he recognized the shift in weight to her right side. She knew she'd screwed up. "I don't want to believe it, but why would someone set you up?"

Adriana threw up her hands. "Oh, I don't know. Maybe a jealous wife? Maybe an unhappy Dom? Maybe a drunk I rejected? It's not like I'm an angel, but I'm smart enough to know which side my bread is buttered on. I don't bite the hand that feeds me!" She slammed her hand down on the desk.

Kendra's face cracked. "Shit, Adriana. What am I supposed to do here? Now I have two threats against Poker Flat because of you. If the resort goes under, everyone's out of a job and the nudists are out a top-notch resort."

Wade moved next to her. He sensed the same vulnerability Hunter did. Kendra was in a precarious position.

Adriana's hands found her hips again. "So you want to fire me? After all I have supported you through? The threats to the opening? The owner requirement? Him?" Adriana lifted her chin to indicate Wade.

Kendra's shoulders slumped and she gave a heavy sigh. "I know. I know. But someone wants you gone and they're putting the resort on the line."

Adriana stepped back. "I'll make it easy for you. I don't want to work for someone who doubts me. I'll just leave." She turned toward the door.

Hunter put up his hand and shook his head. "That won't necessarily help unless we can determine that the person who put up that site knows what's happening on the resort and how."

"Wait." Kendra stepped around her desk. "Are you saying someone here could be feeding information to someone beyond the resort?"

He nodded.

Adriana shrugged. "Doesn't matter. I know when I'm not wanted." She brushed by him, striding out the door, but he kept his eyes on Kendra.

Wade came up behind her and put his hands on her shoulders. "We'll figure this out. We haven't come this far to back down now."

She turned her head. "I know. My heart says to do whatever it takes to keep Adriana, but my brain is being realistic. If the resort folds, where is everyone else going to go? Who's going to hire a former madam as their cook? Or a former thief as their waitress? Or an accused arsonist to do their books? Of all my staff, Adriana is the mostly likely to land on her feet. If I fire her, the rest are safe. At least I hope."

Hunter pushed off the doorjamb and shook his head. "If you fire Adriana, I walk. And I'll bet I'm not the only one."

Kendra's eyes widened in surprise, but he ignored her look and left the room.

~~~~~

Adriana lay naked on the lounge chair on her back patio, her eyes closed as her body soaked in the sun's rays. She'd packed her kitchen and deserved a break. Kendra hadn't fired her yet. She had no idea why, but it was probably only a matter of time. Maybe it was because she was still on "vacation" and there could be some rule against firing an employee while they were on vacation.

It didn't really matter. It didn't take a fortune teller to see she would be out of a job soon. She'd packed her living room the day after she and Kendra had it out. She'd tackle her bedroom tomorrow. That Kendra would sacrifice her for the resort hurt, even if she'd probably do the same in her shoes.

But that Kendra had doubted her stabbed far deeper, more than she expected. She'd grown soft living at Poker Flat, where everyone looked out for one another. She needed to figure out what she wanted to do next.

Lacey had come by again and brought her more breakfast. She and Selma still believed in her and wanted her to stay. That was something. But Kendra wasn't completely convinced it was a setup. And who could blame her?

On one hand, Adriana was flattered her boss felt she couldn't have pissed off anyone *that* much, but on the other, that Kendra could believe she'd put Poker Flat in jeopardy stung.

She took a sip of her beer then lay back and closed her eyes. It was weird drinking in the middle of the day while at Poker Flat. By now, she would have the bar open and be serving guests, watching them hang out in the pool, probably would have given Lacey a hard time at least once and made Andrew blush a few times.

It sucked being ostracized. She hadn't even seen Hunter the last couple nights. She didn't have the guts to break into his casita again. He'd given her a pretty serious warning about doing that when he'd checked on her after she stormed out of the office. He seemed pissed, so she'd held back. That he might think she'd put Poker Flat at risk bothered her. Then again, she had no clue what that man thought.

She would have liked to do some online shopping for new toys, but Kendra had insisted on taking her computer as well. "Just to keep anything else from happening." But she wasn't stupid. They were going to try to find out if her computer had been hacked. That was the only reason she was still at Poker Flat. The tiny hope they would figure it out.

She should probably go shopping tomorrow, before she went stir crazy and—

"Uh, Miss Perez?"

She opened her eyes to find Andrew staring at her. Now that was a boost to her bruised ego. She gave him a sultry smile. "Hi, Andy." She bent one knee up and let it angle to the side a bit. As expected, his gaze left her breasts and riveted on her pussy.

This is what she needed, a little worship. "Did you need me for something?" She practically purred the words. She'd be happy to give the young man a blowjob right here just to have a little fun.

His Adam's apple moved as he swallowed hard. "Um, not exactly. I was sent to give you a message."

She grinned. The man couldn't take his eyes from between her thighs. The urge to spread them wide was strong, but she'd never get the message if she did. "And the message is?"

"The people in casita number four wanted to know where you were. When I told them you were on vacation at your place on the resort, they asked me to tell you they were disappointed you haven't stopped by the last two nights."

Huh? That didn't make sense. "How would I know to visit them?"

"They said they gave Hunter the message to give to you."

Now that was interesting. She doubted Hunter forgot. Maybe he was mad at her, or maybe he didn't get good vibes from the foursome. She couldn't be sure which. They *were* a little pushy. "Was that all they wanted?"

Andrew drew in a breath. "No, they said for you to come over this afternoon. They have a surprise for you."

Oh, now that sounded promising. It also would give her something to do with the rest of her day. Something pleasurable. Feeling a bit more like herself, she let her knee fall to the side, opening her pussy more to Andrew's gaze.

The man took a deep breath and his hands fisted at his sides.

Glancing at his jeans, she could see an impressive bulge pushing at his zipper. "Andy, did you want to have a taste?" She moved her hand down toward the narrow slice of clipped hair that pointed to her sheath.

His head bobbed and he took a step forward, but then he halted. "Thank you, but I need to get back to work."

Wow, the man was a cowboy through and through. Taking pity on him, she straightened her leg and crossed it. "Of course. Maybe some other time then."

His gaze came up past her breasts this time and he gave her a grateful grin. "Yes, miss." After tipping his hat, he climbed into the tan golf cart and drove back the way he came.

She couldn't be sure if he was grateful for her invitation or that she had released her hold on him. What bothered her more was that she wasn't even wet. After teasing a man like that and with the anticipation of oral sex, her juices should have been flowing.

Maybe a visit to casita number four was in order. If Hunter had reservations about them then hanging out during the day should be safe with so many people around. And if he was just mad at her, it served him right to take it on himself not to deliver a message.

Happy to have something to do, she jumped up and headed into her casita. The only problem would be disguising herself so none of the staff would recognize her. She may be on vacation, but being caught fraternizing with the guests after that bitch complained could get her in more trouble.

She'd have to go naked to pass as a guest, but her black hair and dove tattoo would be a dead giveaway. She must have something that could disguise her hair, maybe a bandana?

Thankfully, she hadn't packed her bedroom yet. She opened her closet and turned on the light. Most of her clothes were sexy, but one side of her closet was specifically for sex, particularly sex play. Moving hangers one at a time didn't help as all the clothing was too sexy. The cheerleader costume, Viking woman and demon were not going to fly on a nudist resort.

She glanced at the shelf above. "Oh, this could work." She took down the box with the Viking wig. On top was a box labeled accessories. She might find something in there as well. Clipping her hair up, she pulled the wig out of the box and put it on.

"Oh please." Two blonde braids made her look like an idiot. She'd never pass for a guest in that. She threw it back in the box. Hell.

She opened the accessories box. Now this had possibilities.

After rummaging through it, she pulled out three small hoops made to look like nipple and clit piercings, as well as a couple temporary tattoos. She'd put the rose on the side of her breast and the Celtic knot around her belly button.

She also pulled out face paint. It was a little lighter than her skin, but she could mix it with black liquid eyeliner to make it match so she could cover her real tattoo. She'd thought a lot about her dove before having it done. To her, a dove meant peace and that's how she'd felt a year after settling into Mrs. B's, completely at peace with herself.

But she still needed something to hide her hair.

Re-shelving the box with the Viking wig, she looked in a number of others. There was nothing. She shuffled through more hangers, looking for an idea of what she could do when she came across a twenties flapper costume. She must have had a wig with that because she'd never cut her hair. So where did she put it? She always knew where everything was.

She sat on the floor of her closet and tried to remember the last time she'd worn that costume. It was Halloween and she'd had nothing on underneath it. She'd had a short wig, platinum blonde, straight bob. So where was it?

Note to self: label boxes with more detail.

"Think, Adriana. What else could you have worn it for? If not a flapper then what?" Was it Halloween or sex play or Mardi Gras? "Mardi Gras! That's it!" She jumped up and ran into her bedroom to grab a chair. Standing on it in her closet, she pulled down a box. She'd never been into Valentine's Day, but she was all about Mardi Gras where anonymous sex was the norm, at least in her circles.

She opened the box. The wig sat on top. She quickly pulled it over her head and looked in her mirror. "Well hello there, honey." It was perfect. Of course, to be a blonde it meant her little arrow of hair to her pussy would have to go. But that was okay as it would allow the hoop on her clit to show.

She immediately walked into the bathroom and took care of that issue. She rubbed her fingers over the smooth skin. She felt sexy all over again. It'd been years since she'd shaved *everything*.

Without a second thought, she pasted on the tattoos, clipped the hoops to her nipples and clit, and mixed up the heavy costume makeup. Standing in front of her three-way mirror, she checked all sides. She stilled as her gaze landed on the tiny red marks left from the whipping. At least it looked as if she wouldn't scar. She had Hunter to thank for that.

What would he think of her like this? A need to know built, but she squashed it. For all she knew, he didn't even want to talk to her anymore. Better to go where she was wanted. Finishing her inspection of her look, she smirked. "Perfect."

Grabbing up one of the resort's towels, she switched on her outside light just in case she was back after sunset and locked her door behind her. Finally, some fun to forget about her troubles.

Hunter loved riding with Julie. She was a very capable horsewoman, which was no surprise since she'd competed in Western Pleasure. As they stopped by the stream that ran along the mountain base, he dismounted and lifted her down. Damn, it was good to be home. It was like dating, learning each other all over again.

She'd grown even more beautiful while he was gone. She was also more timid around him. Part of that was his stupid dreams at night. But he was sure they would fade the longer he was around her.

After checking the ground for critters they might disturb, he spread the blanket and put the small wicker basket on it for her. As she sat and emptied the contents, he brought the horses to a shadier spot were wild grass grew.

When he turned back, he had to pause and drink in the peaceful picture of the scene. His wife's wavy brown hair lifted with the slight breeze as she focused on laying out their lunch. A saguaro cactus rose up behind her on the other side of the stream like a sentinel and the purple-flowered thorn bush to the right made her appear so delicate.

He took a deep breath of the dry air. He should pick a flower for her and put it in her hair. That's what he used to do. He strode toward her, his intention to bring her that flower, but instead he crouched down next to her and lifted her chin with his fingers. "I love you."

She smiled shyly. "I love you, too."

Ignoring the food she'd spread out, he lowered his lips to hers, his need to reclaim her too strong. He sensed her hesitancy. It was as if she was afraid of him and it rankled. It took all his willpower to pull back and sit.

Her smile returned as she handed him his sandwich and a bottle of beer.

He needed to take it slow, but he didn't want to. He was too happy to be alive.

The burn of the M16 bullets as they hit his calves swept through his nervous system and his leg twitched.

Immediately, her brows lowered in concern. "Are you okay?"

"I'm fine." He looked away. He wasn't fine. He wanted her. He wanted to feel alive again.

Wait, he hadn't been wounded in his legs after his first tour. He was fine to make love to his wife. He wasn't messed up. He was supposed to be proud and ready to celebrate. But now he was scarred in so many ways and he needed to find peace.

He pulled her against him, ignoring her squeak and kissed her, pushing her lips open so he could taste her sweetness.

But the taste was exotic, like cinnamon, and as he grasped her silky hair, he breathed in the scent of sage. She pushed her body against him and moaned. She wanted him as much as he wanted her.

Finally.

He pushed her back on the blanket and covered her with his body.

Her hips tilted toward him and ground against his hardening cock.

Shit, he needed to be inside her bad. He bunched up her split skirt, thankful to find no panties barred his way. With one hand, he unzipped his jeans and let his cock loose.

Her breathy voice echoed in his head. "Now."

Yes, now. He pushed her legs wider and set his cock at her wet entrance. Thank God she was ready because he had to be inside her.

He pushed his cock home in one quick glide, holding his position tight against her.

Another moan sounded in his ears and her pelvis pushed up against him as if she couldn't get enough.

He pulled out and pumped back in, starting the age old movement that would bring him to bliss. He wanted bliss.

But he didn't deserve it. He'd left his wife for another tour. He'd protected a general instead of her. He was alive and she was dead.

The woman beneath him laughed. "Now this is heaven."

He leveraged himself up, his cock still inside her and stared into lively brown eyes.

"Do it."

He wanted to resist. His brain said no, but his body was in control. Against his will he pulled out again and slammed back in.

"Yes!" Laughter followed.

He did it again and again, rocking Adriana's body as he buried himself deep inside.

Her joy resounded in his ears, making him feel as her pussy sucked at him, forcing the beginning of pleasure to radiate outward from his groin.

She chanted as he rocked into her. "Yes. Yes. Live. Live."

No. He couldn't. But he was and his body tensed as her scream filled his ears and her sheath tightened around him, forcing his pleasure to explode.

Hunter opened his eyes to see the ceiling fan above his head. His body was covered in sweat and the sheets were soaked with come.

"Fuck."

CHAPTER SEVEN

Hunter rubbed the side of his face. That dream was the weirdest yet.

He glanced at the clock. It was four in the afternoon. Close enough. He rolled out of bed and walked into the bathroom. Turning on the shower, he stepped in and let the warm water calm his racing heart. He leaned his forehead against the shower wall.

She was making him feel good again. He didn't want to feel good. He liked his anger. He deserved his pain. Why was she doing this?

An image of the shattered sliding glass door flashed across his mind. Fuck.

He'd been safe, the glass a barrier between watching and feeling. Then he had to go and break the glass. Now he knew what she tasted like, how she smelled, and the warmth of her body. He also had come to know her thoughts and her lust for life.

She was the bullseye and he was the bullet racing toward it, refusing to be redirected.

This sucked. Staying away from her wasn't helping. Nothing helped. His control was slipping, over his need, his anger, his life. He had to take back control.

He moved his head beneath the spray and poured shampoo in his hand. As he washed what little hair he had, he threw out one plan after another to gain control.

As he lathered his body, it hit him. Maybe he needed to roll with it and through it, like taking a punch. Go with the momentum, let it take him into the motion and out. It might work. The only problem was, he wasn't sure where exactly *out* would be.

He turned the water off and quickly dried himself. At least he could move forward on his private investigation. His friend had been delayed in getting to him because there were far too many things of greater importance, but once he'd focused on the source of the photo site, he'd been able to track it no problem, except it initiated from an office complex, and there were at least twenty business located there.

Hunter donned his black jeans and boots. He checked his face in the mirror. He needed a shave, but he wanted to take advantage of waking early and get to the main building before five.

Opening his closet, he pulled out a black, long-sleeve shirt and threw it on. He grabbed his hat and glanced at the slider on his way out to make sure the bar he cut to fit was still in place. Everything was secure. After locking both the door and the new deadbolt, he headed for the reception desk.

He tipped his hat to two couples walking toward the stables. They were probably going for the sunset trail ride. He still couldn't see how riding a horse naked could be comfortable, even though Wade assured him they kept the horses to a walk. Frankly, he didn't consider that "riding," but for nude vacationers, it was probably a dream come true.

Walking into the building, his stride slowed. Lacey was not at the desk. Did she leave already? Damn, but it wasn't five yet. He continued down the employee hallway to the back room. There he found her putting paper packets away in a cupboard.

His relief caught him by surprise. What was another day?

It was a delay his reawakened investigative abilities would not be happy with. He enjoyed this challenge. It reminded him of his days on the force and his first tour overseas. It gave him a sense of purpose, but more than that, he felt on top of his game. Energized. Happy.

No, not that, just productive.

"Lacey, I need your help."

She started as he spoke. "Oh, Hunter." Her hand covered her chest. "You scared me. What are you doing up so early? Nothing's wrong, is it?"

"No."

"That's a good thing." She closed the cabinet. "What can I help you with?"

He stepped back to the door and closed it then turned to face her. "What kind of information do you collect on guests when they make their reservations?"

She leaned back against the counter. "I get their name, address, phone number and credit card. Why?"

"I need all that information on every guest who has stayed here over the last month when the judge was here in order of most recent to oldest."

Lacey's eyes widened. "I don't know if I can do that. That's very sensitive information."

"And I'm in charge of the security of this place. If I can't keep it secret then we might as well close the place down."

Lacey's lips formed a self-deprecating smile. "Good point." She clasped her hands in front of her. "But I should probably ask Kendra first."

"No." He needed to make Lacey an ally. "Do you think Adriana is innocent?"

"Of course."

"Then you need to keep this between you and me."

"But Kendra is just concerned about the resort. I'm sure she'd want to help. It's not like she's fired her."

He looked away. He needed that information and if he had to break into Lacey's computer, it might take days. Shit. "The reason Kendra hasn't fired Adriana is because I told her if she did, I would walk."

"What?" Lacey took a step forward to grasp the chair tucked against the table. "Why would you do that?"

Because Adriana was innocent. Because she didn't deserve to be fired. *Because he didn't want her to leave.* No, because it wasn't right. "Justice. It's about getting justice. Adriana doesn't deserve to be fired without further investigation. If I uncover proof she set up the site and was paid for those photos, then fine. She should be fired."

"You don't think she did it either, do you?" Lacey's gaze was intense.

"No, I don't. It's not how she operates."

"Exactly! And Kendra knows that too. So why does she want to get rid of her?"

That was easy. "This is Kendra's dream. If she gets rid of

Adriana then she no longer has a problem and Poker Flat stands a chance of surviving. Kendra is thinking of all of us who would lose our jobs and not be able to find employment anywhere else." Including him.

Lacey's shoulders fell. "That's true, but Adriana has done so much for Poker Flat. It's not right."

"No, it isn't, so will you help me?"

She glanced at the clock. "I should be able to pull that up and get it printing, but I have to leave because Cole and I are going out. You'll have to wait for the print to finish and shut down my computer for me."

"I can do that." He stepped back from the opening that led to the front desk area.

Lacey nodded and walked through.

This was just the first step, but if he could find someone who worked at a company in that office complex, he might just find the true culprit. Then all he needed was the person's relationship to Adriana and their motivation.

He followed Lacey into the front, his blood pumping with renewed purpose.

It took her no time to pull up the report. Once it started printing, she gave him a stern look with a quick lecture about turning off her computer so no one could get into it. He swallowed his smile and nodded.

Apparently that did it, and she was headed out the front door.

He didn't need anything else from her computer. The only thing of interest to him would be Adriana's background, but everyone who worked on the resort already knew that. She was more than happy to share.

And that's why he was so certain she hadn't set up the site to sell photos. He and Kendra had gone through every photo on Adriana's cell phone but they didn't find a single picture of a guest. Kendra wasn't surprised and neither was he. He had the feeling Kendra wished they had. It would make it a lot easier if she'd been betrayed by her staff like she had once before.

But he'd found it very telling that none of the guests were in Adriana's photos. The only pictures were her with other staff, some x-rated selfies in a three-way mirror, and the rest were pictures of her former dog and her car. There were no pictures of the girls she worked with at the bordello or of her old boss.

It said a lot about her. As open as she was, she never let anyone get close. A phrase from a poem he'd read in high school that had been resonating with him lately came to mind. "No man is an island." Adriana appeared to be an island.

It made his existence to date appear full and yet *she* seemed to be the one full of life and himself half dead. But he had loved... and lost. The pain in his heart would always be there, but at least he had known what it was like to give his heart and hold someone else's.

Guilt niggled at his brain. His parents loved him as well. So did his siblings and he'd shut them out, his pain too much to bear, barely contacting them over the last year. He dug his phone out of his pocket and scrolled through a couple dozen photos.

If he died tomorrow, these people would mourn him despite the fact he hadn't talked to any of them in over a month. He hadn't told them where he worked or lived to keep them from visiting. He should call them soon.

If Adriana died tomorrow, who would mourn her? Lacey,

Selma, Andrew, Jorge, Wade and even Kendra. Probably the old man who used to work here too, Billy. That was it.

And himself.

Yes, he would, but she wasn't about to die. She was about to be fired if he didn't figure out who wanted her to lose her position. Would they continue to make her life miserable if she was let go? How would they know?

The printer stopped printing, so he picked up the sheets and looked around for a stapler. He didn't want to lose any of these leads. The desk was as clean as Adriana's car was messy. Yet he'd heard these two were good friends.

Shaking his head, he opened the top right hand drawer and pulled out the stapler, not in the least surprised it was there. He used it and returned it to where it belonged. Then he turned back to Lacey's computer and closed down the program she'd used. On her dashboard screen were icons for three nudist forums.

He stilled. That had to be it! That's how a person would know whether Adriana still worked at Poker Flat or not. If their main goal was to have her fired, they could nonchalantly ask if she was still there. He clicked one of the forums. A page of topics came up.

He opened one that looked promising. Shit, there had to be two hundred responses. The eight pages in his hand looked to be a whole lot quicker than the forums, plus on forums people could have user names that had nothing to do with who they really were.

Closing out the forum, he shut down the computer and glanced at the clock. He still had a good thirty minutes before his shift started. He rolled the papers up and strode out of the room. He'd start tonight and then finish after work, hopefully.

As he headed for the fork in the dirt road, he noticed a blonde guest turning down the path to the staff casitas. That wasn't good. He picked up the pace to catch up to her.

Adriana sat on a chair with a gin and tonic in hand as she watched Patti, Steve and their friends have sex. The afternoon had been fun, drinking a little, flirting a lot, and joking. These were her kind of people, open about sex and how much they liked it.

They even exchanged sex stories, but she hadn't been turned on by them, so she jumped on Patti's friend's suggestion she watch "the experts." They were definitely obliging and she could tell they loved being exhibitionists.

Patti, who was on all fours with her friend's husband pumping into her from behind, wasn't too busy giving her own husband a blowjob to glance her way. Steve was on his back, eating out the other man's wife, while the wife played with her breasts, showing them off to her own husband who kept glancing at Adriana as well.

She made the appropriate faces, hoping her unease didn't show. Something was seriously wrong with her. She wasn't even wet yet. Hell, a porn movie made her wetter than she was now.

This job thing was really cramping her life. That had to be it. It was either that or the knowledge that Hunter didn't work during the day and therefore wouldn't be watching from outside. It didn't matter because she didn't plan to hang around after dark.

Though the two couples were nice, they were pushy and made clear exactly what they expected next. She needed to beat a hasty retreat, but she had to have a good excuse. They all knew she wasn't working so that wouldn't fly. Would having a date work? No, they'd tell her to have him join them.

The two women started to moan in earnest, their eyes closing as the men brought them to their orgasm. She watched, waiting for the man behind Patti to close his eyes.

As soon as he did, she quietly stood and slipped around the corner into the living room. Grabbing her keys, which she'd left on the coffee table, she palmed them to keep them quiet. The slider was open, so she raced out and ran up the path toward the main building. Yeah, it was pathetic, but she had more important matters to worry about.

She just needed to crest the ledge and slip around the main building. Finally, she was safe.

"Excuse me. There's nothing for guests that way."

She stopped and a slow smile curved her lips. She had no idea why Hunter was already on the job, but it would be great to see exactly how good a cop he was. Slowly, she turned around, careful not to move naturally.

He strode toward her. When he reached her, he hooked her arm in his, turned her back the way she'd been walking and continued that way. "Adriana, what are you doing out in the guest area?"

She pouted. "How'd you know it was me?"

When he didn't answer she looked at him. "Well?"

He shook his head at her. "Because I know you that's how."

She gave him a sexy smile. "But you don't 'know' me in the Biblical sense…yet."

His mouth actually quirked upward just a smidge. Score one for her.

"You didn't answer my question. What were you doing among the guests?" He propelled her toward her casita and since that was where she was headed anyway, she happily complied. "I was visiting. I guess you forgot to give me the message from the foursome the last couple nights, but Andy drove his golf cart right out here to let me know they were upset because I hadn't visited them."

"That wasn't a very good idea. What if Kendra or the couple who caused your forced vacation to start with had seen you?"

"Aren't they gone yet?"

"No. They leave tomorrow." They had reached her door and he released her arm.

"That's why I was disguised. Don't you think I did a good job?" She opened her arms to make sure he saw her nipple hoops.

He actually looked this time, letting his gaze roam over her body. "You shaved."

Holy crap, she was getting wet. "I did. Do you like it?"

His gaze returned to her face. "Do you?"

"Yes. It's been a long time since I shaved everything. Do you want to feel?"

He stepped up to her and cupped her between her thighs, his fingers pressing against the tiny hoop clipped to her clit.

Her heart shifted into overdrive and her stomach tensed with anticipation.

He rubbed his thumb over her mons. "Silky."

She swallowed. "Inside is too." She expected him to pull back, but instead one of his fingers burrowed between her labia and slid into her opening.

"Oh."

"You're wet. Guess your afternoon was pleasurable." The hard edge in his voice made her uncomfortable.

"Actually, I only watched. Just another live porn movie."

His finger remained buried deep, but it was the only place they connected. Even her breasts weren't touching his shirt. She wanted them to. She touched his top button to play with it, hoping to open it, but he dropped the papers he'd been holding and grabbed her hand.

"You're playing with fire."

She lowered her head and looked up at him from the side. "I *am* fire."

His gray eyes turned dark, like storm clouds. "Then we may as well burn together." With his finger still inside her and her hand in his, he pushed her backward until the outside wall of her casita kept her from going any farther.

As the rough surface connected with her bare back, her pussy flooded with anticipation.

Hunter's lips turned upward into a grin that promised she would be taken right now. He lifted her hand in his over her head, but still didn't touch her anywhere else. "I hope you like it fast and furious."

Her breath caught in her throat. Holy crap, he wasn't teasing! Every nerve ending in her body came alive. She barely got her breath through her throat. "Yes."

"Good." His mouth came down on hers and his tongue foraged through her mouth like a man on a mission to claim her.

She wanted to touch him, but forced her free arm to remain at her side, her instinct telling her he had to be in control of this if she wanted him to finish and not leave her hanging. He had that ability, that control. The thought of him leaving her halfway through kept her in check, allowing him to take what he wanted from her.

Her tongue tangled with his, tasting the mint of toothpaste as she inhaled the musky scent that was all him. But she didn't make any aggressive moves, not even to sweep inside his mouth like she wanted to. Knowing she would enjoy this without giving anything had her libido revving. She moaned in surrender.

The soft vocal sound did it.

He pressed his body against her naked one, the bulge in his jeans pushing against her shaved mons above his hand. His finger inside her didn't move. It was as if he held her against the wall with it and that was its only purpose.

He continued his onslaught on her mouth as he pressed his chest against her breasts. Her nipples, already hard, ached as the cotton shirt rubbed them, the hoops adding extra stimulus.

Usually she would demand, direct, even take matters into her own hands, but she didn't, letting him have full rein. It was incredibly stimulating and her sheath instinctually tightened around his finger.

His hand holding her there clamped harder in response as he broke the kiss. He didn't say anything, just looked at her lips.

She couldn't resist. She licked them.

The slightest tic in his cheek was his only reaction before he backed up a step and lowered his head to her nipple.

Oh yes. With her hand stretched above her, she tilted her head back against the warm, rough surface and let him have his way.

His teeth latched on the hoop held there by a clip and yanked it off. Her knees wobbled and she pushed her butt against the wall harder to keep herself standing. His hand around her wrist above her head tightened, but he didn't lift his head away.

Instead, he nibbled lightly at her sensitized tip before swirling his tongue around it. Her nipple ached with need. He pulled it between his teeth, which had her moaning again as the heady feelings zapped down to her core.

He sucked her nipple into his mouth completely and pulled hard, causing her to arch as her sheath contracted around his finger. She wanted to scream that she needed his cock inside her now, that she'd waited long enough, but she clamped her jaw tight. She didn't want to risk him stopping.

His finger inside her moved then. Not in and out but side to side, as if testing her ability to take him. She purposefully relaxed her sheath, though it was the hardest thing to do while he sucked her nipple.

His head came up and he looked at her. "I'm going to take you now."

Before she could register his words, his finger left her and she heard the sound of his jeans zipper.

Hell, he was going to screw her out here, in the sunset, against the wall of her casita. It started a fire inside her so fast, she thought she'd come right then.

But the idea was no match for the reality. He still held one of her hands above her head, as if he'd forgotten he did so. Or maybe it was his symbol of control. It didn't matter to her as he used his other hand to press his cock head against her pussy.

His knee pushed one of her legs aside, opening her up to him. He teased her for a moment as he rubbed his cock from her opening up to her clit, brushing the hoop and moving back. His hand on her wrist tightened again just before he pushed his cock into her, bringing his body flat against her, causing her breath to catch as need swept through her.

She stared at his neck, watching his pulse beat hard as the blood flowed down to fill his cock inside her.

She wanted to sigh with relief, but there was no relief. It was only more teasing. Pinned between him and the rough wall with his cock mostly inside her, she wanted to scream with her need.

Her stomach was tight with pleasure and she squeezed him in her sheath.

He leaned back and stared into her eyes again. Lowering her hand, he wrapped it around his neck at the same time he clasped her other one and wrapped it around as well.

Her breathing came out in little pants as her anticipation built. Usually with a man, she'd make a sexy comment to make him move, but she kept quiet.

"On two, hook your legs around my waist. Ready?"

She nodded as a thrill raced straight to her pussy.

"One. T—" He'd leaned them away from the wall, grasped her ass, and bending his knees, slammed his cock to the hilt.

The zing that rocketed through her took her breath before she was lifted up. She forced her legs to wrap around his waist. They fell back against the wall and he moved even deeper as he pressed her against it.

Oh freakin-a, she was going to come any second now. How was that possible?

"Adriana, look at me." His voice was not only its usual low tone, but husky with need.

Her gaze met his and the lust in his eyes almost sent her over the edge.

"Now." It wasn't a question.

It was a warning and one she was relieved to hear. "Yes."

His eyes closed as his hips moved back and his cock slid out only to bury itself deep inside her. As it hit her cervix, her world erupted. She screamed as every pleasurable sensation collided inside only to sweep out of her as if it burst beyond her body and into the cooling air.

He continued to pump into her, rocking her against the abrasive wall, keeping her semi-aware state going. Each pump prolonged her ecstasy as her orgasm began to subside then strengthened again with each thrust.

A groan, from deep in Hunter's throat, traveled up his chest and escaped as if he'd tried to hold it back. "Argh."

He came, his semen heating her up from the inside, adding one final spark on the fire.

Beyond grateful for the first real orgasm she'd had in a long time, she grasped him hard, around the neck and between her thighs, contracting her sheath to make it great for him as his hips slowed, until a final push into her.

She held tight as her breathing slowed. Opening her eyes, she gazed at the sky filled with bright oranges and pinks and grinned. She felt as if those colors were the same inside her satisfied body. Still orange from the heat, but turning pink, flush with relief.

Note to self: have sex at sunset, outside, more often.

Hunter leaned against her as his breathing slowed, but he didn't lift his head.

"I don't think I could walk." She sighed. "My knees are beyond weak."

He didn't move or respond.

She ran her hand over the back of his neck, the buzzed hair at his nape shorter than the scruff on his chin. It was soft but prickly. Kind of exciting. "I guess you'll just have to walk your beat with me attached to you all night."

That did get a response, though not what she'd expected. The man snorted.

Finally, he leaned away and looked at her. "Mac might raise her eyebrow, but I doubt any of the guests would be surprised."

She laughed, too satisfied to contain it. "I guess you're late for work now, huh?"

He glanced at the sky and shrugged.

"Yeah, I don't want to move either, but I should let you go. I know keeping the resort safe is important."

He didn't respond. Instead, he stared at her as if he were trying to figure something out. His gaze wasn't intense, but it did make her uncomfortable, so she let one foot slide down to touch the ground.

Hunter's eyes closed as her movement changed the configuration of her sheath.

Reluctantly, she let her other foot touch the ground. Better to get it over with quickly. Taking a breath, she slid her ass down the wall. Her knees really did give way then and she held on to his neck and chuckled. "Told you."

He finally reacted, a self-satisfied grin of pride lifting his lips. "Lean against the wall."

She smiled seductively. "Thought I already had."

He shook his head as she released his neck and let her back take a lot of her balance.

He bent over and lifted her keys from the ground where she must have dropped them. Crap, she didn't even remember letting them go.

Hunter opened her door and dropped her keys inside. He came back out and lifted her in his arms.

"Oh, my. Now this is new. I like this." She wrapped her arms around his neck, ignoring his surprised look at her statement.

He walked into her casita and deposited her on her love seat. Then he strode into her kitchen and grabbed a bottle of water from her fridge. He handed it to her. "Drink."

Okay, she could do that. She took the bottle and opened it, enjoying the view of his still semi-hard cock sticking out of his jeans.

He tipped the bottle toward her mouth.

"Okay, okay." Once she'd taken a swallow, he walked into her bathroom.

When he came out, he was all zipped up.

Bummer.

He stopped in front of her. "Finish that whole bottle. We were outside and your body is going to need the hydration." Then he cupped her face, leaned over and kissed her, no tongue.

When he'd finished shocking her, he left, locking the door behind him.

Adriana stared at the door. She wanted him to come back.

What was with that?

Chapter Eight

Hunter grabbed up the papers he'd dropped on the ground outside Adriana's casita. He was damn lucky a wind hadn't come up. So much for research tonight.

Stopping by his casita, he dropped off the sensitive information and grabbed a protein shake on his way out.

Every muscle in his body felt good. He hadn't realized how badly he needed a woman. Or maybe it was just Adriana. The woman was sexy personified and her taste was intoxicating.

The image of himself licking between her legs rose up and started his cock hardening again. Shit. He really wanted to do that and have a hundred other sexual encounters with her.

That short blonde wig against Adriana's dusky skin had been just a bit more than he could resist. The whole look, like a bad girl for the taking, had fed his hunger. At least he'd already planned to give in to his need and see where it took him.

His concern was that it appeared to be taking him to another bout of sex with her. She'd been perfect. Tight, expressive, ready, and she orgasmed faster than he did when he'd been sure he was going to leave her in the dust. How the fuck did she last so long with the guests?

His gut tightened at the thought of her revisiting that foursome. He'd tell her it wasn't a good idea. She should—"Shit." He hadn't even used a condom. As soon as he got off shift, they needed to talk.

He'd swing by after his patrol and wake her up for a good morning tussle. He stilled. He wanted her again. He wanted to wake her up by making love to her slowly this time, if that was even possible with her.

He'd just reached the fork in the dirt road when Mac flagged him down. He strode over to her. "What's up?"

She cocked her thumb over her shoulder. "I had a complaint from one of the guests. They decided to take a walk to the barn to get away from some yelling that was going on in casita number four."

"That's the foursome. Did the woman relate what the yelling was about?"

Mac shook her head. "No, but she said two women were screaming in a very high-pitched tone. I asked her if it could simply be they were having sex, but she was adamant it was an argument and two women were involved."

"I'll take care of it."

"Want me to come with you? In case the women need to talk to another woman?"

"No." He smirked. "If it was two women arguing, my guess is the last thing they need is another woman."

"Okay. Let me know if you need help." Mac gave him a knowing smile. "Women can fight pretty dirty."

He stared at her a moment.

"Just saying." She turned and strode away.

Shaking his head at the implications of Mac's statement, he headed for the other side of the resort.

The lights inside the main building could be seen clearly as he walked by. He glanced at the horizon before heading down the path to the guest casitas. The sky had turned a lavender-gray as darkness settled over the resort.

He didn't hear any yelling now, but he should check in and find out what the problem was. Guests couldn't be disturbing other guests.

As he approached the casita, he could see a couple sitting on the patio. They both had a glass of wine and appeared to be talking amicably.

"Good evening."

They looked startled by his greeting. That wasn't that unusual. Very few people kept abreast of what was going on around them *all* the time.

"Hi, there." The blonde woman gave him a smile before letting her gaze drift down his body.

Once again he was happy his job required him to be clothed.

Her husband put down his wineglass. "You're Hunter, right?"

He nodded. "I understand there was quite a bit of yelling going on over here."

The blonde flushed, but her husband addressed him. "Patti and Cindy got into an argument. It was nothing. I'm sorry if it disturbed anyone."

Hunter steadied his gaze on Patti. "It did. Some of the guests strolled over to the stables just to get away from the noise."

Patti's chin came up. "I'm sorry, but Cindy was trying to blame me for scaring off Adriana when it was clearly her fault."

Scaring off Adriana? This woman obviously didn't know Adriana very well. "Why do you think someone scared her off?" It was none of his business, but the statement had been too odd not to delve further.

Patti looked at her husband then back at him. "Because according to the forums, Adriana enjoys sex with swingers, but she has to be in charge. Since she scooted out of here just as the four of us had reached our first orgasm, I knew it was because we pissed her off by not letting her be in charge."

Patti's husband jumped in. "Cindy suggested Adriana watch in case she wanted to get the feel for us, but my wife had suggested she be involved."

Hunter nodded seriously to keep from bursting out in laughter. He took a moment to give them both a serious stare until he was sure he had his humor under control. "Adriana left because she had an appointment with me."

The couple looked at each other in surprise. Patti was the first to recover. "Well, shit. We didn't think she had work stuff to do since she was on vacation this week."

His humor over her term "work stuff" vanished. Their knowledge of Adriana's schedule concerned him. "How'd you know she was on vacation?"

Patti shrugged. "The forum. There's a whole thread on Adriana. We were being overly cautious after what happened last weekend."

Hunter's gut tightened. Was every second of Adriana's life being discussed on a forum? He kept his irritation at bay. "Which forum is that thread on?"

Patti crinkled her nose. "I'm not sure. I'd have to look it up."

He stared at her.

"Let me get my laptop." As she walked into the casita, her husband addressed him.

"Is something wrong?"

"No, I just want to make sure Adriana is aware of this particular forum since she is being discussed."

The husband relaxed. "Oh, I'm sure she's aware of it. She's actually quite the star. Our lifestyle choice is not very common, so to learn about such a vivacious woman, who works at a nudist resort no less, is very exciting. We probably should have invited her over after dinner instead of in the afternoon. We brought our new sex swing with us just so she could try it. Since she's single, we figured she probably didn't have one. It's not every day a couple lugs one of these with them on vacation."

Hunter barely kept his fingers from curling up. Instead, he concentrated on his breathing so as not to say something that would definitely piss off this guest.

"Here it is." Patti came out with the laptop open. She stepped next to him to show him. He had to lower his head because she was very short.

"Oh here, you can hold it."

He took the laptop from her and studied the URL first. It was a Swingers forum. He doubted Lacey had this one.

"Hey, Patti, this means you can make up with Cindy."

The blonde squealed. "You're right. Let's do that right now."

Her husband stood. "You can look through that and just leave it in our casita. We need to get up to the dining room before our friends leave."

Patti grinned. "Yeah, if we can't trust the resort's security, who can we trust? Thank you so much for coming over here."

Before he knew what she was about, she pulled his shoulder toward her and kissed his cheek. "Come on, Steve."

The couple grabbed their towels and power-walked up the path to the main building.

Hunter took the opportunity to review the forum. The thread with the most topics was titled Adriana. He opened it and stared. Subjects ranged from "hot, hot, hot Hispanic" to "gang bang honey."

He opened one and read. It was a detailed account of having sex with Adriana. He closed it quickly and skimmed the topics again. One caught his eye. "Dom, Dom, sub and more." His jaw tensed as he opened it. Sure enough, it was a description of the night he'd busted in the casita. There was no mention of him, but Adriana was made out to be a bitch. The responses were mixed. Some clearly sided with Adriana. Others sided with the Dom. The user name was Dds4love.

Hunter closed out the topic and checked the URL again. Memorizing it, he shut down the computer. There was no way he'd give this to Lacey. It looked like he would need to do a lot more research and his gut told him it was going to piss him off.

Closing the laptop, he walked into the casita and placed it in the kitchen, out of view of any of the windows or doors. As he left, he closed the slider the couple had left open. They must expect him to watch over everything. Then again, Poker Flat hadn't had anything stolen on the resort since he and Mac had come on board. Just proved the Dom incident was not the norm.

Leaving casita number four, he continued his patrol around

the guest quarters before walking up to the main building. He headed around toward the pool when a conversation caught his attention.

"Did you hear? Someone p-posted pictures of guests from here on a website. Rumor is it was a staff person." The young woman's voice sounded familiar.

"Oh my Lord, who could it be?" The older woman was obviously shocked.

"I r-read on the forum that it might be Adriana. I just couldn't imagine. I mean, if she's that hard up for c-cash, why not just go back to s-selling herself."

Hunter clamped his jaw hard.

"I can't believe that of Adriana. She's such a sweetheart."

"Well, I g-guess you never know. Good thing the site went down. I'd hate to have my p-picture up there, even if I am a swinger."

"Oh, we don't do that." The older woman's voice sounded more concerned over swinging than photos. She must be a nudist only.

"Have a g-good night." The young woman strode off, her unsteady steps clear in the quiet of the night. He also heard her husband with her.

That was definitely Patti. Her speech pattern, tone of voice when drunk, and her reference to swinging confirmed it. There was only four swingers at the resort this week.

She was definitely worth a closer look.

After checking the garage, he came back to the fork and strode toward Mac's area. He wanted to confer with her. He didn't see her, so he started with the brand new Old West town. It wasn't exactly a town since it consisted of only one side of what would have been a main street, but it was pretty convincing.

He stepped onto the boardwalk to look into the windows of the store fronts. There was a mercantile, a sheriff's office, saloon, bank and separated, but in line, was a blacksmith hut. He'd just stepped toward the swinging doors of the saloon when a foot came out of nowhere to trip him up.

He quickly jumped as the body that owned the foot landed on the wood beneath the batwing doors.

He chuckled, offering his hand. "Is that how you treat a guest who is wondering around at night?"

Mac grabbed on and pulled herself up. "Guests aren't that quiet. You have damn fast reflexes."

"The military will do that to you."

Mac shrugged. Obviously, that wasn't where she'd learned her skills. Her comment about women fighting dirty had his balls itching. Wherever she learned to fight, he'd bet it included moves he'd never think to use.

"Were you looking for me?" Mac brushed off her sweats.

"Yes, I just discovered I have a shitload of computer investigation to do. There is a swinger forum with a whole thread about Adriana. There has to be over three hundred topics in it, and the Dom that whipped her the other night has posts on there. I need to read everything he's posted."

Mac looked askance at him. "Everything?"

He took a deep breath. "Yes."

"That might not be a good idea, Hunter. Would you like me to read through it and tell you what I find?"

"N—" He shut his mouth. Mac wasn't Lacey. She'd seen Adriana's activities herself and hadn't made a judgment about them nor appeared squeamish.

"It might help your investigation if someone looked through them with an objective eye. I can always copy and paste the posts I think important." She raised an eyebrow in question.

He still wanted to say no, but reading this Dom's comments on Adriana's exploits would definitely throw his objectivity right out the window. "Actually, that would save me time. I have a whole list of guests over the last month I need to research."

"I'd be happy to help." Mac smiled. "I don't want to see Adriana leave here any more than you do."

"Good. I'll take the whole resort tonight while you work on this on your computer."

"I'll have a report for you by tomorrow's shift."

Hunter gave her the URL and took over her patrol around the Old West town as she headed back to her casita to get started. After covering the stable manager's office, he strode into the stables.

They often covered each other for nights off, but being in the stable after his strange dream this afternoon had him hankering for a ride. He stopped by Elsa's stall. The Arabian was badly scarred from a wildfire years ago, but Wade had bought her from Lacey's husband. They ran a horse rescue ranch.

Did Adriana ride? He could see her up on Elsa in a pair of jeans and a tied-at-the-waist half-shirt. Elsa poked her nose over the stall door. He gave her a pet. "Sorry, girl. I don't have anything sweet for you."

Romeo next door heard him and looked over his door too. Hunter moved to him. The large quarter horse was impressive. He was another from Lacey and Cole's ranch, but Hunter didn't know his story. "Would you like to go for a ride?"

The horse looked at him expectantly, and he stroked the side of his face. It had been too long since he'd ridden. He hadn't even had the urge until now. It was as if he were waking up. It felt wrong, like he ignored Julie's death by feeling human again, but it wouldn't stop and he knew exactly who to blame.

Adriana.

After a long night of getting his priorities straight, Hunter headed back to his casita. He'd stopped by Adriana's around midnight on purpose. Since he was in the middle of his shift, he couldn't have sex with her. That he'd still struggled with keeping his hands off her proved how attracted he was.

Luckily, she was on birth control, used condoms with the guests, and was tested once a month to make sure she didn't have any sexually transmitted diseases. Her life in the bordello had ingrained good habits she said she couldn't break, except with him.

Her obvious confusion over that fact just fed his manly pride. Shit, he had reason to feel that way. Here was a woman who usually had sex with three to four people at a time and he'd had her coming within minutes.

Unlocking his door, he picked up the guest information and threw it on the kitchen counter that separated that room from the living area. He opened his laptop, which he kept plugged in there and turned it on.

While he waited for it to boot up, he opened the fridge and stared at the protein shakes. That wasn't going to do it if he stayed up later than usual. Pulling out the eggs, cheese and onions, he set himself up to make an omelet. He had frozen Italian sausage in the freezer, so he took it out and set it in the microwave to defrost.

Adriana had offered to cook him breakfast. Maybe he should

take her up on that. Better yet, follow that with an hour in his bed. He grinned. Damn, if he didn't feel more like his old self. It was strange, and guilt squashed his good mood.

He needed to focus on the guest list. If he couldn't even protect Adriana, he was as worthless as he originally thought. Dumping his omelet on a plate, he grabbed a fork and walked around the counter to sit on a stool.

Pulling the laptop around to face him, he brought up a browser and started searching the names on the list, beginning with those guests still at the resort.

Two hours later, he rubbed his eyes and tried to focus on the screen, but it was hopeless. He needed sleep. So far he had more suspects than he'd thought possible. Too many local nudists worked in the damn office complex. They probably ran into each other there and chatted about Poker Flat. Hopefully, Mac could help him narrow that down with what she found in the forums.

Picking up his dirty plate, he stuck it in the sink and covered it in water. He'd start the dishwasher when he woke up. Stripping as he walked to his bedroom, he dumped his clothes in the full laundry basket. Damn, since when did he live in such a mess?

Putting that out of his mind, he crawled into bed and focused on an image of the moonlit desert he'd enjoyed while on patrol, but the vision of Adriana coming in his arms kept intruding. "Shit."

Rolling over, he punched his pillow down. Again, the vision of her head thrown back, eyes closed and mouth open in a loud scream as the pinks from the sky bathed her in their glow, invaded his mind.

He could feel her sheath squeeze as her fulfillment took over.

There was no way his mind would go anywhere else. If he

wanted to sleep, he had to give in to it. He allowed the image to morph into having her in his bed like he'd originally wanted to. In no time, he drifted off, making love to her.

Hunter's alarm went off early so he could do more research before his shift. Feeling unusually rested, he shaved and showered. There was something about Adriana that canceled out all negative memories and feelings. He didn't like it because he didn't deserve it, yet he gravitated to her.

Once dressed, he opened the laptop. Without Mac's information, he could be wasting his time, especially if she was able to narrow it down. He hoped it wasn't just the threesome with the Dom that bashed Adriana because only one of them worked in the office complex and it wasn't the Dom. A narrower search would take a lot less time. If that forum was reporting Adriana still had her job then whoever was trying to frame her might become more aggressive. The sooner they found the culprit the better.

He glanced out his sliders, which showed it was still bright, but the sun would soon set.

Fuck. He closed the laptop and stuffed his keys in his pocket. He moved around the counter and threw lunch meat, cheese, bread, strawberries and a couple bottles of water into a plastic bag. On the way out the door, he grabbed up his rifle. His need to be with Adriana was too strong.

Hunter strode down past the two casitas separating his from hers. He wished she lived next door now when weeks ago he was glad to have a few buildings between them. He shook his head at himself.

As he approached, he heard swearing coming from inside since she had most of her windows open. He strode around back to her slider to find it wide open as well. The woman was very trusting.

As he stepped into her living room, his lips quirked. Adriana had a mouth like an infantryman.

"You better fucking fit in there you cock-sucking motherfucker or I'm going to make you wish you were the fibers of a Goddamn rug."

He moved to the door of her bedroom to find her sitting on a liquor box overflowing with material of some sort, in her signature cut off jean short shorts and sleeveless white button-down shirt tied under her breasts. He leaned against the doorframe, cradling the rifle in his arm. "What are you doing?"

Adriana jumped up and stared at him. "Holy Hell, where the devil did you come from?"

He nodded toward her slider. "From your patio."

She stared for a moment before comprehension dawned. "I forgot to close it, huh?"

He nodded. "Why are you swearing at a box?"

"I'm trying to pack as many clothes as possible into it. My car won't hold that many boxes so they have to be full."

He looked back toward the living room and scanned the boxes already packed and labeled. There was no way those would all fit in her car.

Shit, she was planning to move. But he could play dumb. "Why are you packing?"

She looked at him like he was an idiot. "Duh, I'm probably going to get fired if you can't find anything to prove I didn't set up the photo site, so I figured I'd get a jump on it." She paused to put a hand on her hip. "You haven't found anything have you?"

The hope in her voice wasn't disguised by her stance. "Actually, I did. I have a friend who was able to track the site's IP address to a location. Now I just have to narrow down who at the location set it up."

"That's good, right?"

For one tough bartender, Adriana's vulnerability showed through. She loved Poker Flat. Every masculine instinct flooded his psyche. He would exonerate her, no matter what. "Yes, that's good. But it will probably take a day or two more before we figure out who the culprit is."

"We?"

He gave her a half grin. "There are a lot of people who work on this resort who are pulling for you."

She turned away quickly and dragged the box to a spot against the wall with two others that also weren't taped closed. "I always said Kendra's misfits were special."

He leaned the rifle against the doorjamb, dropped the bag of food on the floor, and closed the distance between them in seconds. "Hey." He lifted her chin, forcing her to stand straight. "Would you like to have dinner in the desert with me?"

Her eyes were misty, proving him right. She'd been touched by her coworkers caring. She didn't want to be an island again.

Unable to resist, he kissed her.

Gently, he brought their lips together until she opened for him. He explored her taste with his tongue, taking time to enjoy every nuance that was her. He held her against him, but not with the sexual fervor of before. He wanted to give her comfort.

She broke off the kiss and looked at him in puzzlement. "You want to go on a picnic?"

"Duh." He threw her word back at her in jest. "Would that be what dinner in the desert was called?"

She smirked. "Hmm, I've never been on a picnic. Sounds good, as long as it includes dessert." She winked.

Hunter's cock reacted and his lips quirked up. "I did bring strawberries."

Adriana rolled her eyes as she stepped out of his embrace. "Really? Good. I can think of a dozen ways those could be fun."

Shit, now his cock was definitely getting hard.

She stepped over to her bed. "Is what I'm wearing okay, or should I put on something more exciting, like this?"

Adriana lifted a three-piece chain from the bed and held two ends up and placed them against her cloth-covered nipples. The third end of chain dangled between her thighs, its clip sparkling with a rhinestone.

Hunter swallowed hard and forced himself not to adjust his jeans. "No, what you have on is fine. It's nothing fancy."

She pouted and dropped the chain. Then a secret smile curved her lips as she reached for something else on the bed. She lifted a headband with black cat ears and stuck them on her head. Without hesitating, she brought a sheer black body stocking against her length. "Maybe you need protection from wild animals?" She lifted a furry cat tail with a butt plug at the end. "I can be a panther and protect you."

Shit, his cock was harder than the desert after a three-year drought. "No." He turned away from the sexy image that was Adriana and picked up his rifle. "I've got everything we need." Holding it up for her to see, he grabbed the bag of food from the floor. "Protection and food. I'll wait outside."

He strode from the casita without a backward glance. If he didn't leave right then, he'd have taken her on her bed piled with clothes, and dinner would have been completely forgotten.

But he wanted something different. He'd been quick last time and with a woman as hot as Adriana, he wanted to savor every sensation. A nice ride, some conversation, a simple meal and an Arizona sunset were what he had in mind before making love to her in the middle of their natural surroundings.

He heard the slider close and be locked. He grinned, pleased she was taking her safety seriously. When she stepped outside to lock the front door, she'd added cowboy boots and hat to her ensemble, which was perfect.

"Okay, cowboy, so where are we going to picnic?"

"Down the trail."

"Great." She looked around. "Um, where's your golf cart?"

He frowned. "We're not taking a golf cart. We're riding."

Adriana's eyes widened. "Riding what?"

He chuckled. "Horses, what else?"

She stared at him for a moment before she shook her head. "Horses? I've never ridden a horse."

With everyone wearing western clothes every day, it was easy to forget it was just the resort uniform. "Now's your chance."

"Really?" Adriana's face looked like a kid who'd just been told she'd have thirty dollars to buy whatever candy she wanted. "Like hold the reins and gallop away?"

He grinned, glad he could help her have a brand new experience. "Yes on the reins, but for your first time, I think galloping might be a little dangerous."

"Hell, what are we waiting for? Let's go." She took the food bag from him, looped her arm around his, and pulled.

He willingly went with her, vaguely wondering what the staff would say about this little excursion before his shift. Then again, it didn't really matter. They were a tight knit group and it probably wouldn't go any further than one another.

With his guess that it was a Poker Flat guest who was out to get Adriana fired, he just didn't want the resort's clientele to know any more about her than they already did.

When they arrived at the barn, Jorge met them. The first generation Mexican-American had taken over the stables after Wade was promoted to resort manager. From what Hunter had gathered, that was the same time Wade had begun sleeping with the boss, but who was he to judge?

Jorge did a great job and would give his life for the horses. He was shorter than Hunter, with short black hair and a crooked nose that rumor had it he received after being in a fight to defend Kendra's honor. The man was thin, the kind of cowboy that had wiry strength even though he was more than ten years Hunter's senior.

He had five horses saddled and ready. "What can I do you for, Cash?"

Adriana laughed that Jorge used the name Cole had bestowed on him, but he just smiled. "We need a couple horses for a short ride."

Jorge looked at Adriana. "So you're finally gonna try it?"

"Absolutely! I'm on vacation, after all."

Jorge gave her a smile. "Good for you, *Chica*. It's about time." He returned his attention to Hunter. "I have two couples coming out for a sunset ride, but you can choose from who's left, except for Ace. He's feeling a little under the weather today."

"Got it." Hunter headed into the barn while Adriana chatted with Jorge. He stepped up to Romeo. "Hey, boy. You ready for a mellow ride?"

The tall quarter horse came over to let Hunter pet him. "What do you say we bring Elsa along for my pretty lady?"

At the mention of her name, Elsa came to her stall door. "I guess that's a yes." He grinned as he walked over to the tack room. Bringing out a saddle and halter for Romeo, he had the horse cinched up and ready to go in no time. It was amazing how it all came back to him, though it had been years since he'd ridden.

As he headed back to grab a halter and saddle for Elsa, the old feeling of loss and hopelessness settled in again. All his horses were gone. His ranch was gone. Everything sold so he could pay for Julie's medical bills, but every expert in the state still couldn't keep her from dying. "Brain dead" they called it.

But he'd felt her squeeze his hand when he talked to her. Sometimes he swore she was dreaming because her eyelashes fluttered. And it wasn't like they had her hooked up to a bunch of machines, just one to help her breathe and she was fed through a tube. Otherwise, she looked as if she slept.

It was his mom who had talked him into saying goodbye. She said if it was meant to be, Julie would hang on and come out of it. He'd been so sure she would. Either that or he just needed her to. Finally, one night when they were alone, he told her she could go if that's what she wanted. He told her how much he loved her and reminded her of some of the fun times they had and the stupid things he'd done to capture her attention.

He'd held her hand and kissed her as he lied through his teeth and told her he'd be okay, but he hadn't really believed she'd leave him.

Two hours later, Julie slipped away.

He'd been shocked.

When the heart monitor went flat, the nurses ran in, but with tears running down his face, he waved them away. He'd signed the DNR the day before, again because he didn't think Julie would really leave him, and since he'd lied to her, telling her it was okay to go, he couldn't go back on his word.

He rested his head on her leg, held her hand and bawled his eyes out. After an hour, the hospital called his mom and she forced him to sit up and say his final goodbye.

The gaping hole in his heart was still there. He should have never gone for the second tour. If she hadn't been driving to meet him at the airport, she wouldn't have been killed.

His fault. His failure.

CHAPTER NINE

"Hey, cowboy, are you just going to stand there all night looking drop-dead gorgeous or are you going to show me how to ride one of these beauties?" Adriana sauntered into the barn, her eyes sparkling with excitement.

He hefted the saddle that he'd let slide to the barn floor and moved to Elsa's stall. What the fuck was he doing? Why was he with this woman?

Adriana moved to the horse's stall. "Am I going to ride you, pretty girl?" She stroked Elsa along the side of her neck. "You'll be nice, right? I've never done this before, just so you know. It's my first time, so go easy on me."

Adriana's unease made him swallow his suggestion they forget the whole thing. He'd told her he'd take her on this stupid picnic, so he would.

She glanced at him, still petting the horse. "I can't remember the last time I said it was my first time." She gave him a lopsided grin, one that made it clear she was out of her element on this, but wanted to learn.

"You need to let me bring her out."

Adriana stepped away. "Okay, just tell me what to do, or not to do. I don't have a clue."

He led Elsa out. "Don't stand behind the horse. They have a kick that could actually kill you."

Adriana moved to the opposite stalls, which were empty at the moment. Shit, now he had her afraid of them.

Great, he was an ass. He focused on getting the saddle on Elsa and cinched it tight. He was about to call Adriana over when he noticed her shorts. Where the fuck was his head? She'd be rubbed raw if he let her ride like that. Why hadn't he had her change? She'd even asked him if she should, but he'd been thinking with his cock instead of his head.

Wait a minute. They offered naked riding at Poker Flat. He strode toward the entrance to examine the four horses waiting to be ridden. Each one had a saddle cover of soft material that stretched over the seat and had a slit for the stirrups with a flap to cover the stirrup leather. It was ingenious actually, and his respect for Kendra went up a notch.

"Need something, Cash?" Jorge sat in a lawn chair just outside the barn smoking a cigar as he waited for the guests.

"Yes. Where can I find one of these covers?"

Jorge smiled. "Pretty snazzy, huh? They're on the second shelf on the left in the tack room."

He tipped his hat. "Thanks."

"And if you're going to want privacy, take one of the left-hand trails. I'll be taking guests up the right one." Jorge winked.

Hunter gave him a quick nod and strode back into the barn.

"Everything okay?" Adriana's smile was tentative. "I mean, if you don't want to do this, that's fine."

Here was his out. He could walk away from spending the next couple hours with her, but he couldn't do that. Getting her hopes up then bailing out was not his way. "No, just need something first."

He continued to the tack room. What the fuck was wrong with him? This was his idea and now he didn't want to go? He was more messed up than he thought. Pulling a saddle cover from the shelf, he returned to Elsa. After pulling the strings tight that kept the material on, he finally understood how they could offer naked riding.

He beckoned Adriana over. "You will want to mount a horse from her left side."

She listened intently to every word he said, nodding as he explained how to direct the horse and slow it down. Finally, he helped her mount.

Adriana looked around. "This is higher than I expected." The worry in her voice was clear. "There's no seatbelt on this?" She actually looked behind her to check the saddle.

He stifled a chuckle. "It's like riding a motorcycle. No seat belt."

"What about a helmet?"

"I can check the tack room. I wouldn't be surprised if there were some in there."

"Are we going to go fast?"

He studied her. She held the reins in one hand, but she clutched the saddle horn with the other. It was the first time he'd seen her look uneasy.

"No, I will keep it to a walk this time." He kept his voice low like he would to soothe a wounded soldier.

She gave him a nod. "Then I'll stick to my cowgirl hat."

He had to give her credit. She was nervous but determined.

He mounted Romeo, the feel of having a horse beneath him again an instant relaxant. He should have done this long ago.

"Oh my." Adriana had her hand over her heart.

"What?" He scanned her to make sure he hadn't screwed something up. "Everything alright?"

"More than alright." Her gaze roamed over him. "You really do know what you're doing."

Her admiration had his male ego rearing its head again. He put a lid on it. "Elsa will naturally follow Romeo, so unless she tries to go off the trail, just enjoy the ride."

"I plan to." Adriana winked, a clear indication she was thinking of a different ride.

He ignored his cock's movement and started Romeo out the barn. He looked back to see Elsa following, but Adriana's eyes were wide.

Holy shit. It hit him. She wasn't making innuendos because she was interested in sex. She used sex to hide her fear. She used sex to keep her distance. As contradictory as it sounded, his gut told him he was right.

When they came outside, the guests had arrived for their sunset trail ride and waved, causing Jorge to stop his instructions and turn around. "Enjoy your ride."

This time Adriana laughed, but it wasn't her usual relaxed one. "Oh, I plan to."

Hunter continued to walk Romeo to the trailhead clearly marked by a wooden sign with a horse's head burnt into it. The sun was definitely lower now, but sunset was still awhile off.

He looked back to check on Elsa and Adriana. Elsa was doing fine, but Adriana seemed surprised.

When she saw him looking at her, she smiled wide. "I didn't realize how much hip action there was in riding a horse. I should have worn my split panties with the center string of pearls."

Aw, fuck. He turned back around, his swelling cock very uncomfortable with the ride. Maybe Adriana just used sex for everything, good and bad.

When he came to the first fork in the trail, he stayed left as Jorge suggested. He really didn't feel like socializing with the guests. Shit, he didn't even feel like talking to Adriana.

As he walked Romeo between a dense grove of mesquite trees and a steep ravine wall, they came out into an area that looked made for a picnic. The little creek was running steadily after recent rains and the desert had started blooming with yellow sun cups, hot pink fairydusters, and a smattering of blue dicks. He didn't plan to tell Adriana the name of those particular flowers.

"Oh wow, look at this." She brought Elsa along beside him as if she'd ridden for years. "Are these wildflowers?"

He nodded. "This will make as good a place as any for dinner."

She didn't say anything, so he looked over at her. She was smiling from ear to ear.

Not sure why she was so happy, he dismounted and came over to her. "Now swing your right leg over without hitting Elsa's rump while holding on to the saddle horn, then lower yourself slowly."

He held the reins and stood nearby, waiting to catch her if she fell.

She dismounted perfectly. "Oh, I am definitely going to have to take up riding. Maybe you could give me lessons." She batted her eyelashes at him before laughing out loud.

He gripped Elsa's reins to avoid taking Adriana in his arms and kissing her. She was a life magnet, enticing him with her exuberation.

He didn't reply. Instead, he led Romeo and Elsa to the stream in case they wanted to drink. It hadn't been a strenuous walk for the horses, but the desert air was dry so it couldn't hurt.

He pulled the food from the saddle bags on Romeo and looked back toward the trail.

Adriana was walking through the wildflowers. She picked each one and smelled it before sticking it into her hair below her hat. They weren't staying. They slowly slipped through, creating a cascade of color on one side of her face.

The woman's sexiness appeared exaggerated in the natural setting. Her long legs in her short cowboy boots just begged him to spread them.

He tore his gaze away and pulled out the rough blanket he'd found in the tack room. At least he'd thought to bring it or they'd be sitting on the dirt. He untied his rifle as well and brought that to a relatively clear spot. Leaning his gun between the branches of a palo verde tree, he spread the blanket and dropped the bag on it.

Adriana joined him, plopping her ass down next to the bag and opening it. "Hmm, not exactly fine dining, but it's a picnic." She pulled out the bread, meat, cheese, waters and strawberries then she tipped the bag upside down and shook. She looked at him. "That's it?"

He shrugged as he sat cross-legged on the blanket. "It's the best you get on the spur of the moment."

She pouted. "And here I thought you'd been planning this all day. But a girl can't be picky."

She made short work of making up the sandwiches, using the plastic bag as her table. She handed him one.

"Thanks."

"Anytime, cowboy." She wiggled her brows before looking down to create her own sandwich.

He'd wolfed down half of his by time she finished making her own.

"Damn, you're one hungry hombre. Let me know if you need another sandwich."

He would definitely need another, but he could make it himself. He wasn't going to have her interrupt her meal to wait on him.

They sat in silence for a while, eating their dinner and watching the butterflies and occasional bee flit between the flowers. There were other flying insects as well, but not nearly as colorful.

He finished his first sandwich and started making his second.

"Hey, I can do that for you."

"No, I know how. You eat."

"Because I need my energy?" She gave him a seductive look.

Shit, if she could make him horny over a ham sandwich, what would he do when it came to the strawberries?

He'd just started his second sandwich when she turned her attention to the luscious fruit. "Did I tell you these are my favorite fruit or was it sheer luck that you brought them?" She opened the plastic box and took one out, but stared at him.

He swallowed his mouthful. "Just luck."

"Very good luck, I'd say." She held on to the green leaves at the end of the strawberry and bit into it, her lips almost matching the redness of the fruit.

He couldn't take his gaze from her mouth, his body tensing over the pure sensuousness of her action.

When she bit off the rest of the fruit and dropped the green leaves on the bag, he turned back to his sandwich, even though his hunger for food had disappeared.

Adriana held a strawberry out to him. "Open up."

Two could play at this game. He opened his mouth and she eased the strawberry in. He made as if to close it then leaned forward and enveloped her fingers and pulled.

Her eyes widened, even as their warm brown irises darkened. She released the strawberry and pulled her fingers from his mouth. "You're being naughty."

He positioned the strawberry in his mouth to bite off the leafy end and spit it out onto the desert floor. He chewed the sweet fruit, losing all appetite for the rest of his sandwich.

Adriana took her time to enjoy each strawberry, occasionally feeding one to him. Her half-lidded eyes and sage scent drew him in. His cock was hard and he wanted in her pants, but he didn't want a repeat of the other day. Hard and fast was not his norm. At least it never had been.

To break the seductive aura she created around them, he took a bite of the sandwich he no longer wanted. He swallowed and gulped down some water. "Why did you join the bordello?"

The question had barely formed in his mind when it came out his mouth, and he kicked himself for asking, especially when she gave him a startled look.

"It's complicated." She bit another strawberry in half.

Now that it was out there, he couldn't let it go. "I have time."

She gave him a disgruntled face and shrugged. "In junior high school, I discovered I was very popular with the boys and a pariah to the girls. By time I was thirteen, I'd lost my virginity to a fifteen-year-old."

He stifled his surprise, careful not show any reaction. His instinct told him she was looking for a judgment she could argue with. When he didn't say anything, she continued.

"It was my first time and his, and we didn't have a clue about what we were doing, but we liked it enough to try again. We finally got it right and it was good, but there was something missing for me."

"An orgasm?"

She nodded. "How'd you know?"

He smirked. "I was nineteen before I figured out that women didn't have one just because I did."

She laughed. "A lot of boys in my high school didn't get that. After dating a few, of course I got a reputation, especially from the girls who now hated me with a passion. I was by far the most unique-looking girl in school."

He didn't doubt that for an instant.

"I decided I didn't need the crap at school, so I stopped dating classmates. I started cocktail waitressing when I was sixteen. Of course, on paper I was bussing tables." She winked. "But I could make over a hundred dollars a night in tips. That was a huge amount of money for someone my age."

Shit, if he'd made that much when he was sixteen, he'd have been in heaven.

"It didn't take me long to figure out I could make a hell of a lot more if I took some of the men up on their offers. Even then I wouldn't sleep with a man who was married or had a girlfriend, but at that age, I was still naïve and thought it was fun."

"What did your mother say?"

Adriana's face closed up, the first time he'd ever seen that happen and it fired up his curiosity.

"There wasn't much she could say. I did my own thing by then. She was always a doormat. Pretty, but no backbone at all."

"Did your father know?"

Her face paled so much at the mention of her father that his gut tightened, afraid of what he'd hear next.

"He was dead. He died when I was eight."

"Heart attack?"

She swayed and he steadied her. With his other hand, he shoved her water bottle at her. "Drink. It's still hot out here."

She did as he suggested, but her color didn't return.

He was an ass for not telling her to forget it, but he wanted to know what had made her who she was. He didn't question why, he just had to know.

She screwed the cap back on the water bottle. "He was working with coyotes to smuggle people into the US. Things went south. He probably didn't pay them all the money he owed them or something. They killed him. It wasn't pretty."

His body tensed with protectiveness as he imagined what Adriana, the child, must have witnessed. "You're lucky they didn't hurt you."

"I hid as soon as the door busted in. Even then I was smarter than my mother."

He wanted to pull her into his arms. He understood. He

needed her to know that. "I've seen a lot overseas. It can be hard to live with. Some guys can't function at all when they get back. Others, like me, make it through somehow, but the dreams can really mess you up." He looked away from her. "It changes you. You aren't the person you were before something like that happens."

Images of the men he'd carried to waiting helicopters came unbidden to his mind. They were still breathing, but blood was everywhere. Sometimes another soldier would run up, before the chopper went airborne, to make sure they had the limb or finger or whatever physical piece of the wounded man was missing. None of them wanted to leave any part of themselves behind.

But the fact was, they did. The first time he left his naiveté and innocence. The second time, he left his pride and his peace.

Her hand on his arm snapped him out of the dark path he'd gone down. They were talking about her.

He had to ask. "When did you decide to make a career of sex?" He figured that was the most diplomatic way to put it.

She grinned, clearly pleased with herself and her color returned. "Oh, that's easy. I was eighteen and agreed to meet this guy after work, to make that extra money. He was from Nevada and I was in Southern California at the time where prostitution is illegal. I hadn't been caught, but the police had started nosing around."

She took another strawberry and bit it in half, taking her time to chew it and swallow, her lips mesmerizing him as they moved.

"Anyway, this particular guy was a hunk from Reno and I was shocked he had to pay for it. When I got into his car behind the gas station, I gave him a condom and told him he had to wear it. He laughed and told me I should be in Nevada where they had whole counties where prostitution was legal.

I tucked that away in my brain, thinking I'd look into it, but that night, with him, I had my first orgasm. I was so thrilled, I offered to service him all the way back to Nevada if he'd take me with him. He did."

She finished off a strawberry and took a sip of water. Hunter had a dozen questions he wanted to ask, but it was always best to let a suspect ramble. She wasn't a suspect in his mind, but the techniques he'd learned on the force had come in handy more than once.

"As it turned out, he was a regular at Mrs. B's. He said he paid for it there because the girls got to choose who they wanted to do and he knew they were clean. I think that's what he liked about me." Adriana gave him a sly look. "You liked that, too."

He nodded, but still didn't interrupt.

"He also liked it because he enjoyed sex, but women he'd been with always wanted a relationship and he just wasn't there. I'm so thankful he was honest with me because he clarified exactly how I'd always felt. Sex is fun, but why did it have to come with all the baggage? I mean, I was eighteen and he was twenty-two. So I figured if he could go to Mrs. B's to have sex and avoid a relationship, then I could work there for the same reason."

His mind whirred with all she'd revealed. His therapists' words echoed in his head about avoidance issues, but they never said anything about sex being used that way. She looked expectantly at him.

"If you were happy there, why did you leave?"

Adriana shrugged, showing more of her cleavage with the movement, and he wasn't oblivious.

"When Kendra asked me to come here, I'd been at the bordello for over ten years and I figured it had served its purpose. I was ready for a change."

He gave her a devilish grin of his own. "But you still love sex."

"You can say that again, and again and again." She laughed. He liked her laugh. It wasn't just uninhibited, it was a full throated, husky laugh that made him feel good again.

She eyed him shrewdly. "So when are you going to show me that body of yours?"

He tensed. "It's not a pretty sight."

She waved his comment aside. "Oh please. I've already seen most of the back side and it was hot."

He frowned. "When did you see my back side?"

Adriana's smile faded. "The second time I broke into your casita. I haven't done it again. I know you're pretty touchy about that. Remember, I fell asleep on your love seat?"

She waited for him to nod.

"You were having a bad dream, so I crawled into bed with you. When you calmed down, I left." She lifted her chin, daring him to make something of it.

Shit, he was too shocked to be angry with her. He'd never had anyone remain unscathed after touching him during one of his nightmares. Even the nurses in the hospital in Germany had called him "Biene" or bee because of his tattoo and because if they tried to wake him up from his nightmare, he came out of it swinging. They finally left him to wrestle his personal demons on his own.

He should thank her, but he just couldn't make his mouth move as he attempted to grasp that she'd made them go away. That had to mean something.

Her look of defiance changed to concern as both her chin and brows lowered. "You have a lot of nightmares?"

He looked away and shrugged.

"I used to have them after my father died, but I think I grew out of them, mostly."

He turned back to her at that. Her brown eyes reminded him of maple syrup, but they weren't sweet, just filled with compassion. This was the Adriana beneath the brash façade. He cupped her face with his hand and brought his lips within an inch of hers. "I need you."

She inhaled at his words, but she closed the distance between them and kissed him. It was a tentative kiss before he parted his lips and let her take the lead. She didn't rush it. Her arms wrapped around his neck and she deepened the kiss, making it sensual… and caring?

He moved his hands to her waist as she sat, her legs bent and to the side. He wanted to keep this new Adriana with him, find out what she was like. He stroked her back where it was bare, enjoying the feel of her smooth skin.

When she pulled back, she gave him a shy smirk, but it wasn't the practiced one she always used. "I want to see you, no matter how imperfect you are."

His gut tensed. "No woman has seen me since I came home. Are you sure it's what you want?"

She nodded. "Yes."

He took a deep breath and nodded.

Her hands moved to the buttons on his shirt, undoing them one by one. When she reached the spot where it was tucked into his jeans, she stopped and placed her hands on his stomach. Slowly, she spread them up his torso, taking the shirt with them.

His body came alive at her touch, starved for the feeling. He closed his eyes, letting his body communicate to him its joy as she moved the material over his shoulders. Was it animal instinct or psychological need that caused such bliss?

"Nice." Her voice was husky.

He opened his eyes as she moved her hands back down over his chest and across his abdominals. When she reached his jeans, again her gaze came up to meet his. Appreciation shone in her eyes.

"I have to see it all." She pulled her legs under her to kneel and unbuttoned his cuffs. First, she smoothed the material down until his hands were free, then she ran her hands from his shoulders to his wrists.

He grasped her hands in his, intertwining their fingers. It had been so long since he'd had his skin touched, stroked. He wanted to savor every second. He raised his right hand with hers clasped in it and kissed her knuckles, bringing her gaze from his body back to his face.

Uncertainty flashed in her eyes before she looked at his left arm and turned that hand within hers. "Oh wow. I love this tat."

He glanced down at his arm and grimaced at the five inch by four inch angry bee tattoo. "Really?"

She laughed. "Yes, really. Why the mean bee?"

"Let's just say it was a leftover from my brief rodeo days."

She shook her head and peered at it closer. "Uh-uh. I want the full story."

"It's not much of a story. I was a scrawny kid back then, but for some reason every time I got on a bull, the damn thing went nuts, as in, more than usual. My friends teased me that I was like a bee and I stung every bull I rode. No one wanted to ride after me because they couldn't stay on for more than a second."

She finally lifted her head. "But he has something in his hands."

He turned his arm away. "Boxing gloves."

She gave him a sly smile. "And…"

"The teasing got bad until I couldn't walk by without the guys buzzing at me. One day, after a particularly bad ride, the wrong guy buzzed and I popped him one. Laid him out cold. It was a stupid thing to do, but I was pretty proud of myself. That night, my friends talked me into getting the tattoo."

"I think it's sexy."

"Of course you do. What girl wouldn't think an angry bee with boxing gloves was sexy?"

She gave him a quick kiss on the lips, squeezing his hands at the same time. "You are one hot cowboy with that mean tattoo, black hat and no shirt, but as tempting as you are right now, I'm determined to see *all* of you, so…" She raised her hands with his. "You have to let me go for that."

His mouth quirked. She'd made it clear she was not a submissive. He didn't want a submissive. He wanted to share their bodies, not take her over like he had the last time. He released her hands, curious what she would do next.

She surprised him. Instead of reaching for his belt, she undid the buttons on her own shirt and slipped it off. Her breasts were perfect, but natural. Not too high on her chest, but full with dark-colored areolas that just begged for his attention.

His cock began to grow, but the need to have her chest pressing against his made it difficult to stay still and wait for her.

She threw her hat to the side and ran her fingers over her scalp before flicking her straight hair behind her.

He itched to feel its silkiness across his bare skin.

Then her hands were on his belt buckle, expertly unfastening it and unzipping his jeans.

His hard cock sprang loose.

She cupped it with her hand and leaned over to examine it. With her other hand, she traced the veins that throbbed with need like a palm reader followed a believer's heart line. But there was no heart involved with Adriana. Or was there?

Impressions of her as he'd seen her, pitching in to help Kendra, teasing Andrew, educating Lacey, praising Selma, darted through his mind. These were the people in the pictures on her phone. She was connected to them. She loved them in her way, even if she didn't know it.

In that moment, with her hands cradling his cock, he wanted to be connected to her more than physically.

She released him and tugged on his waistband. "Cowboy, you're going to have to wriggle your butt out of these so I can pull them off."

He shook his head. "Boots come first."

"Tell me about it." With those words, Adriana sat back on her butt and pulled off her own. She wiggled her toes and sighed. "I'm being spoiled this week, not having to wear these all day."

He grabbed one of her feet and pulled it into his lap.

"Hey, what are you doing?" She tried to take her foot back.

"I'm massaging your foot." He slipped off her sock and rubbed his thumb into her arch.

"You're not one of those guys who has a foot fetish, are you?"

She moaned as he moved his fingers over her heel. "I mean it's okay if you are. I just didn't peg you for one."

He chuckled. "No, I have no fetish. From your sigh after taking your boots off, it was obvious you needed a little relief."

She looked at him strangely.

Not having any idea what might be going on inside that mind of hers besides sex, he continued to work on her foot, just inches away from his exposed cock. The difference in their skin color was particularly stark since he'd never been in the sun nude.

When she leaned back and closed her eyes, he set her foot aside and pulled the other onto his lap.

The sun had started to lower and shadows began to invade the ravine on the opposite side of the creek. It was still warm where they sat, but it would turn cooler once the sun set. As he rubbed, he enjoyed the view of Adriana's naked torso. Her darker skin was like an aphrodisiac. The perpetually tan, healthy color called to him, his hands always itching to touch it.

When he finished his massage, he set her foot aside and stretched out his legs.

Adriana opened her eyes. "That was utter heaven."

He toed off one boot. "Haven't you ever had your feet massaged?"

"Yeah, a little, if I get a pedicure, but it's been over a year and my old pedicurist didn't have big strong hands like yours." She wiggled her brow, making the comment a sexual innuendo.

There it was. When he did something nice for her, she made it sexual to hide her discomfort. If he had his way, she was going to be a whole lot more uncomfortable before he started work tonight. The woman needed to know she had value beyond her sex appeal.

He toed off his other boot and stood.

Adriana knelt again, her eyes on his cock.

If she kept her gaze there, he'd have a whole lot harder time keeping this slow. He turned around. Maybe if she saw exactly what she was in for, it would cool her off a bit.

"Hey, are you shy or something? Don't forget, I've already seen your back side, or most of it."

He didn't respond. He just dropped his jeans and stepped out of them.

There was silence behind him.

CHAPTER TEN

She was probably trying to swallow her disgust. He'd seen the backs of his legs. They weren't pretty. After two tours in Afghanistan, two IEDs and a mortar, he had enough scars to qualify as Frankenstein.

His buddies had joked with him that he protected his pretty face, but the fact was, it was pure luck. The back of his head was a real mess.

Adriana's hand on his ass surprised him.

"Crap, you're built." Her voice was husky once again and his cock responded.

He started to turn.

"No, stay like that a minute." Her hands smoothed over his butt and squeezed.

Again, that human touch after so long had his eyes closing in sheer bliss. Her hands made their way across his thighs, squeezing his tense muscles here and there. When they reached his calves, he held his breath, those and the back of his head were the most messed up.

Adriana's hands didn't hesitate, stroking over his muscles there. "Your calves aren't nearly as bad as one of Kendra's."

Surprised by her statement, he turned around.

Adriana's eyes widened and a guttural moan came from the back of her throat. "Freakin-a, Cowboy. I'm going to come just looking at you."

She reached for his thighs, but he caught her hands, and pulled her up to stand in front of him. "I want to feel you against me." He clamped his jaw tight, pissed that he'd said that out loud.

Adriana didn't give him her usual seductive smile. Instead, she pulled her hands from his and unbuttoned her shorts.

Shit. He hadn't meant to reveal that particular need to her. She must think him odd for sure.

When she dropped her shorts to the blanket, she was bare.

As much as he wanted to resist the primal need growing inside him, he was weak. He pulled her body against him and held her there.

Every spot where her soft skin touched his hard body burst with joy. It was the least sexual embrace he'd ever had with a woman while naked before sex.

She laid her head on his shoulder, her silky hair falling against his skin and down her back. He stroked it, revealing in its silky texture. He wanted it against him, everywhere.

He closed his eyes, embracing her warmth and feminine curves. His withdrawal from human contact had been a gradual thing and completely unconscious. Now, he felt like a starved man before a banquet. Taking calming breaths, he held it together.

He felt Adriana tilt her head back and opened his eyes to meet her concerned gaze.

"Hey, you okay?"

He tried to push a word past his suddenly closed throat, but it wouldn't go. He nodded instead and gave her a partial grin.

"Okay, just checking. I wouldn't want you to pass out or anything."

At that, he did chuckle. "Not a chance." Without warning, he scooped her up into his arms and knelt down on the blanket.

"Oh, I could get used to that." She gave him a seductive smile.

He ignored it. No way he would rush this. He lowered her to the blanket and lay down on his side next to her.

She immediately rolled toward him, hooking a leg over his own. Her shaved mons brushed his cock lightly.

He hardened more, anxious to be inside her but determined to take it slow. He pulled her hair over her shoulder and across his body. It was comforting and titillating all at once.

She leaned in and kissed him, but he wouldn't let her inside. Instead, he stroked her back.

Obviously feeling thwarted, she pulled away a couple inches and reached for his cock. He caught her hand and rolled her onto her back, her hair sliding off him to fall onto the blanket.

She looked at him from beneath lowered lashes. "Whoa, looks like my cowboy wants to ride."

The length of his body pressed against hers filled empty places in his psyche, calming his sexual need. He raised an eyebrow. "Looks can be deceiving." He kissed the side of her neck where he'd sucked so hard last time.

He followed that with a kiss to her collarbone, her breast bone, the side of her left breast. Shit, he hadn't even touched that nipple last time they were together. He'd have to remedy that oversight now. After licking the underside of her breast, he moved up to lave her areola until it puckered with need.

As he flicked his tongue against the hard nipple, he glanced up at Adriana's face. Her head lay against the blanket and her eyes were closed. The rise and fall of her chest told him she was excited. He continued his tongue play, circling and flicking.

She arched toward his mouth and her hands gripped his head, sending his hat onto the blanket. "Crap, Hunter."

He smiled inside. Not exactly an endearment, but he understood what she wanted. Gently, he took her hard nub between his teeth and moved his jaw back and forth. Her hands tried to burrow into his hair, but it was far too short for her to grab.

He nibbled first then sucked her nipple into his mouth, not hard, but enough to cause sensation. Once he had it inside, he flicked it with his tongue again.

She moaned, loudly, still trying to push him to rush it.

Moving to her other breast, he repeated the same process, determined to be fair this time. When he'd finished his attentions to her breasts, she was panting. Pleased he could bring her so much pleasure so easily, he continued to lick down her body. He stopped at her belly button where he sucked for a moment, then after licking at the small indentation, he moved down to her shaved mons.

He paused as he caught sight of a dove tattoo, no larger than the head of his bee tat, nestled down on the right side of her mons. He'd never noticed it before. It didn't seem to fit her, but hidden away like it was, it could be a hint of the soft side of Adriana. He kissed it as hope kindled a tiny flame in his heart.

He noticed her hands had stopped moving on his head as if

she waited with anticipation. Her wait would be a bit longer. He moved lower, forcing Adriana's hands to drop from his head.

With his hands on the insides of her knees, he spread her legs farther apart. The shade had caught up to their side of the creek, but it didn't hide the moistness seeping from her nether lips.

His cock, already hard, jerked at the sight.

Adriana lifted her head. "Do you like what you see?" Her attempt at a sexy smile was not successful.

He hoped that was because she was feeling too good to be purposeful in her seduction. "I do, but I'm sure I'm going to like the taste even more."

"Oh, hell." She dropped her head back to the blanket.

He grinned.

Leaning over the juncture of her thighs, he started with her outside labia, licking it from top to bottom. He moved inward, licking first up and down one side before the other. Then he explored her opening, pushing his tongue inside her, curling it up and out to noisily smack his lips as her flavor flowed through his mouth. He thrust inside with his tongue again and let his nose brush across her clit. He felt her knees bend even as her pelvis tilted.

Success buzzed through him, a sensation he hadn't felt in a long time. Bringing Adriana pleasure awakened his instinct to give.

He pulled his tongue from her sheath and licked upward against her clit.

She moaned, "Yes."

Happy to oblige, he thrust inside again and licked her juices over her clit, circling it this time. The hard nub combined with her taste was an aphrodisiac he couldn't get enough of.

Again and again he repeated the action, lost in the sensuous moans Adriana emitted. He wanted her to come. As his tongue took time flicking and circling her clit, he slid two fingers inside her. When her sheath tightened around them, his cock leaked pre-come.

Shit, this was harder than he expected. He continued to play against her clit with his tongue, loving the feel of that hard nub but he didn't move his fingers. Her hips rose off the blanket and her sheath tighten in anticipation of her orgasm.

Quickly, he removed his fingers.

Her hips hit the ground fast, losing contact with his mouth. "Fuck, Hunter. You're killing me."

Her brows were lowered in frustration.

He barely kept a smile from showing. "Don't reach for it. Just relax. I promise, you'll be glad you did."

Her raised brow made it clear she highly doubted him, and this time he couldn't help his chuckle from escaping. "Just lie back and let me do all the work."

She shook her head but let it fall back to the blanket.

He returned to her clit, licking and rubbing, adding a series of nips every once in a while with no set pattern, loving the intake of breath it caused on her part even as her hips undulated and he used his hand to push them down.

Finally, when she began to emit tiny sounds, he placed his hand against her mons and sucked her clit.

"Oh God." Adriana attempted to push up, but he held her still.

She started to whimper, her head rolling back and forth.

Pride filled his veins as he increased and decreased his suction, keeping her near the edge.

"Hunter, your fingers."

He didn't answer. He wanted her sheath empty to increase the intensity of her orgasm and to highlight the difference when he entered her.

Her moans grew loud, echoing off the ravine walls, filling his soul with satisfaction even though his cock ached.

He sucked her clit hard and let go, letting his teeth glide against it.

She shuddered before a scream tore from her.

He repeated the action again and again as she came apart under his mouth, victory making him feel invincible…alive.

She grabbed his head and tugged up.

"Done?" He watched as she shook from her orgasm.

She nodded, her panting probably made it hard to speak.

When she started to shiver, he covered her with his body to keep her warm, careful not to let his weight crush her.

Her forehead had beads of sweat near her hairline, and he gently brushed a stray strand of hair away.

She opened her eyes. "That was crazy good."

"That was the intent."

Adriana's breath caught at the unguarded look in Hunter's eyes. It wasn't need this time, it was caring. Uh-uh, that wasn't part of the program.

She winked at him. "Mission accomplished."

He nodded with supreme male ego.

He wasn't supposed to be *that* good. He wasn't supposed to make her feel more than the physical, and she definitely felt her heart jumping up and down.

It had to be respect. No one person had been able to give her an orgasm like that and for that long. And the man hadn't even come yet. She respected that and his ability to play her body so well.

She pressed her hips toward his. "Your turn."

He shook his head and gave her that devilish smirk. "Not without you."

"Again?" The word escaped before she could hold it back, but she clamped her mouth shut to avoid revealing any more. She could always fake it. No need for him to know the chances of her coming again, especially after that amazing orgasm, were nil.

"Yes, again. Do you doubt me?" He did look a little put out.

She gave him a sly smile. "Let's just say I need to see it to believe it."

"I plan to make a believer out of you, woman."

A thrill raced from her brain to her core at his words. She wasn't sure which part excited her, but she liked it.

Hunter lay above her, his weight on his elbows, his ripped chest brushing her nipples, his abs and pelvis tight against her. She pressed her mons into his hard cock.

He cupped her face and kissed her. It wasn't the gentle kiss of before, but it wasn't the hot kiss he'd given her the first time they had sex. Instead, it was sensual as he tangled his tongue with hers and touched every part of her mouth.

He pressed his cock against her as if to tease, moving his hips in the motion he would soon start inside her.

Surprisingly, her body responded, her belly tensing with anticipation. She wrapped her arms around him and lifted her chest against him. His body was so hard, it looked like all his muscles were tensed and it felt too good against her womanly curves.

One minute she was kissing him, his body covering her so nicely, and the next he'd rolled over, taking her with him and she lay splayed over him. Now this was a position she really liked. Actually, she liked them all, so it was technically the truth.

Hunter released her lips. "I'm guessing here, but it looked like you enjoyed riding."

His wit had her cracking up and she let out a laugh. She made eye contact with him before looking at the horses tied near the stream. "I'm so glad you taught me, but I think I need more practice."

His chuckle vibrated her chest and a ridiculous sense of happiness suffused her at being able to make him laugh. She was supposed to make him come, not laugh, but it *was* fun.

He moved his arms from around her back and dropped them to the blanket. "Practice away."

His grin was catchy and she found herself mirroring it before his words penetrated her brain. "Oh." She sat up onto his thighs, his cock straight up in front of her.

Damn, the man was hard. How he could think she'd find his body anything besides hot baffled her. Then again he did say she was the first woman to see it.

The weight of those words finally penetrated her brain. Crap, he hadn't been with a woman since before he went overseas. She was a hundred percent sure Hunter would never cheat.

That meant the day at her casita had been his first time in how long? Suddenly, riding him well became important. He deserved this. He'd served his country, been wounded, and come home to what? What happened to his wife or was she gone before he left?

"Did you need a different stallion?" Hunter's lips were quirked to the side, but his stormy gray eyes of earlier had lightened and sadness seemed to have pervaded his thoughts.

"Absolutely not. This is the only stallion I want right now. I'm just trying to decide the best way to ride."

He clearly doubted her, so she pushed those heavy thoughts aside. The only one she kept close was that he deserved this.

She laid her hands over his chest and touched every hill and valley made by his strength. Lacey had once described him as a bow about to shoot an arrow and she was right on the money. And she hadn't even seen his body.

Stifling the excitement that kept distracting her, she moved her hands over his shoulders and the bulges of his biceps and forearms. This time when she did it, he didn't capture her hands nor did he close his eyes. Instead, he watched her intently as if he expected her to find something she didn't like.

Freak, there wasn't a single part of the man's body she didn't like. Even his scarred ass was so taut, it caused her sheath to tighten just from looking at it. But his front was almost scar free and far too perfect to be real.

Hmm, maybe she should taste it to be sure. She leaned forward, bracing her hands on the ground and ignoring the hard cock pressed against her abdomen. She licked the hard nipples on his chest, first one then the other, back and forth.

Just as she took one between her teeth, Hunter's hand came up and brushed the side of her breast before settling on her waist. His touch was gentle and he held her loosely, not directing or restraining in any way.

It reminded her of some of the couples who came to Poker Flat. As they walked into the dining room, the man would have his hand on the small of his lady's back. It was a gentle touch, caring, but definitely letting every other man in the room know she was his.

The only other male in the immediate area was Romeo, so she doubted that Hunter was claiming her. She should keep her mind on her task, especially because it was a pleasant one.

Lifting her lips from Hunter's nipple, she couldn't help kissing his scruffy chin. Everything about the man was too sexy to ignore. He watched her as if he couldn't wait to see what she would do next.

She sat up again and felt his thigh muscles shift as her weight pushed down on different places. His thighs were as hard as the cock in front of her, which just made her want him inside her more. So what was she waiting for?

She ran her fingernail along the underside of his erection. He was silky, but his veins stood out as the blood filled his cock to capacity. Moisture gathered between her legs, surprising her. She hadn't even held him yet.

Not willing to question the unbelievable, she held his cock in her hand and stroked down once. With her other hand, she cupped his ball sac, gently rolling it in her hand. When she glanced at Hunter, she found his eyes closed. She much preferred that.

She scooted her hips closer, so he touched her mons. Unable to stop herself, she pressed his cock against her and rubbed the other side. A ripple across his abdomen was the only response that let her know he enjoyed it. The man's control was just plain amazing.

She viewed it as a challenge, though he hadn't said anything to make her think so. Lifting herself up, she pushed his erection forward with her hand, holding the tip and brought her opening to connect with the underside. Then she slid herself forward, brushing her clit over the ridge of his head. Zings of pleasure drove straight to her core and her sheath flooded.

She glided back and moved forward again, enjoying the tease to her pussy, the tingles to her clit and the sight of Hunter's abdomen tensing and releasing with her movements. His hands gently held her hips, making her feel precious.

To have a man affect her in so many ways was unusual. Maybe she *could* have a second orgasm. Lifting herself higher, she positioned Hunter's cock at her opening and waited.

He opened his eyes and looked at her, but didn't say a word. Instead, his hand squeezed her waist lightly before releasing. It was the green light from him, whenever *she* was ready. Hell, he was too nice, too caring.

She broke his gaze and looked down at where they would link together. Slowly, she let him glide inside, his hard, full cock spreading her sheath as it moved deeper until she lowered herself to his hilt. She sat straight up, tilting her hips, but he hit her cervix and she leaned forward just a bit to release that pressure. The man was big and leaning forward was better.

With practiced skill, she began a slow movement up and down, loving the control she had as she angled herself different ways, feeling him push against her in numerous places. The hot pleasure that accompanied every downward movement built in her core. It was sex, hot, stimulating, raw…but it wasn't raw.

Uncertainty filled her at the same time Hunter's other hand clasped her waist and he pushed his hips up.

"Yessss." The word slipped out as she leaned forward more

and pressed her pelvis against him, the pubic hair around his cock brushing against her clit as he filled her with each back and downward motion she made. She panted as everything inside her prepared.

Hunter's hand moved up to cup her neck. "Kiss me."

She let him bring her down against his chest, her nipples pressed into his hard pectorals. She held back even as her pelvis ground against him. He didn't tug at her.

He waited. Her call. Her decision. But it wasn't. The connection between them was more than physical and he'd figured that out before her. She loved being held to him while they continued to thrust and move against each other. She wanted to be even closer, be a part of him.

Giving in to her need, she lowered her face and let her lips touch his. The kiss was passionate as he thrust his tongue into her mouth like his cock thrust between her legs. His hand on her neck held her there while his other wrapped around her back, pulling her tighter against him, like he wanted to crawl inside her.

She wanted him there.

Her clit charged and her sheath filled, her body tensed for her ecstasy. But she held back, her pulse pounding as she waited for him. She had to have him with her. She sucked at his tongue and wrapped her hands around his head, like she could pull him inside her.

Hunter's mouth broke from hers. He grunted once before a yell split the air.

He triggered her orgasm, flooding her with his heat and spinning her world out of control.

She held tight, afraid to let go as elation burst through her like the sun's rays coming over the horizon, blinding everything its beams touched. Hunter, the only solid thing in her universe as her body dissipated into the air in joy.

As her world slowed and her breathing became more regular instead of desperate pants for oxygen, she opened her eyes to find him staring at her, a slight grin on his face and pleasure in his eyes. The pink sky overhead bathed his skin, making him look flush… and happy?

He cupped her head and brought her lips to his for a sweet kiss.

She broke it and lay her head on his shoulder. It had been different. This, what they did, meant something. It wasn't supposed to. It was sex. That's all.

Hunter stroked her hair, the gesture intimate. "You're incredible."

Her? No, she wasn't. She was good—no great—at sex. She didn't qualify for "incredible." That's what lovers said to each other. She and Hunter were…. She searched for a word. Nothing fit.

Desperate to feel normal, she squeezed her sheath.

"Whoa, there. Let a man recover his breath at least." Laughter was clearly in his voice.

She pulled away and sat up. This needed to stop, whatever it was. But even as she contemplated standing up, his hand came down on her waist again.

"What is it? What's wrong?"

She glanced at him to find his brows lowered in concern.

"Nothing. Why?"

"You're afraid."

"I was just giving you a minute, like you asked." She gave him her seductive smile. "But if you want to go again…" She winked for good measure.

He scowled. "Stop. There's nothing wrong with feeling something when two people connect."

She forced her eyes to widen. "Connect? Oh, you mean this?" She pointed to her crotch. "I think we both felt a lot, don't you?"

He continued to frown, but disappointment came into his eyes. "No man is an island."

"What?" Now he was going off the deep end.

"Never mind. We should head back. I need to talk to Mac before I start work."

His hands left her waist, and she swallowed a moan of disappointment. What was wrong with her? This was what she wanted, for him to keep his distance. Wasn't it?

She didn't look at him, not willing to watch his face as she pulled away. She stood, effectively disconnecting them in more ways than one. Looking for her clothes, she found her shorts first and pulled them on, keeping her back to him.

She hadn't even buttoned them when his arm came around her waist and his hand came over her mouth.

He whispered in her ear, "Shh, don't move."

What? If this was some scare tactic…

"Mountain lion."

Oh, crap. She nodded to show she understood.

When he released her, he walked without a sound to his rifle. The man's movements were as smooth as any cat she'd ever seen.

Hunter raised his rifle to something behind her, and she slowly turned her head in that direction. Her knees shook and threatened to buckle as she stared at the cat in the growing darkness, sitting on a small outcropping, no more than ten feet away and just above their heads. Fear that it would pounce on her was the only thing that kept her upright.

The shot rang out and a piece of stone split off from the outcropping just inches under the cat. It turned and leapt up the canyon wall.

"Fuck." She dropped to the blanket, her hand over her heart as she gasped for breath.

Hunter crouched down and laid his hand on her shoulder. "It's okay, he's gone."

She lunged against him, toppling him over, but he grasped her to him as she shook in his arms. She couldn't help it. The animal was beautiful on television, but up close and personal was more than she could handle.

"It's okay." Hunter repeated his words as he rubbed her back with one hand.

Her mind knew that, but her body still needed to catch up. She held on tight, thanking her stars Hunter had thought to bring a gun, had been there, and held her now. What a wimp she was.

She pulled her head back to look at him. "You missed."

He grinned. "No. I didn't want to hurt him, just scare him. This is his home more than ours."

"Oh. Then nice shot." Her heart started to return to normal. "I wonder if Jorge knows we have a mountain lion nearby. I've never heard anyone mention one. I thought you brought the rifle for rattlesnakes."

"I did." He smirked. "I'll tell Jorge and Wade. If a mountain lion has made his home nearby, they may want to close this trail and develop another."

Feeling a bit more like herself, she finally let go of him. "Who's to say? It could be a she?" She started to stand up when she noticed two things. He'd already donned his hat and he had a burr stuck on the bottom of his foot. "Wait, don't move."

He immediately looked behind him.

"No, nothing threatening. Let me see your foot."

Hunter bent his foot to look at it himself.

"You're such a man. Give it to me." Despite his affronted look, he let her have his foot. With her long nails, she carefully extracted the burr and any leftover spikes. "That would have hurt."

He pulled her toward him. "I didn't know you cared."

His kiss was invasive at first, as if he were mad, but it ended tenderly, once again making her uncomfortable. But before she said something stupid, he set her back.

"Better get dressed. We need to go. It's getting too dark to be out here without a light."

That she could understand and quickly pulled on her top, socks and cowboy boots. She picked up her crushed straw cowboy hat. "Guess I'm going to need another one of these. No doubt Lacey will take it out of my pay." She tried to reshape the straw when she remembered her status with Poker Flat. "Then again, I won't be around long enough for that."

Hunter pulled her against him again. "Don't say that. I'm going to find who's doing this. That's why I have to talk to Mac. She was doing some research and we need to compare notes to narrow down our suspect pool."

She shrugged, not wanting him to know how much she was depending on his abilities. "I'm just preparing for the worst and hoping for the best." She gave him a fake smile and stepped over to Elsa.

Hunter followed her over and gave her a hand up. Once situated comfortably in the saddle, she looked around for the lion. "Why didn't the horses warn us?"

Hunter swung his leg over Romeo and pulled him around to face her. Fuck, the man was hot. She wished they could have sex all night.

"The breeze was blowing in the wrong direction. That mountain lion is smart. Now, the horses are skittish because of the gunshot. The sooner we get back the better."

"Lead the way." She waved her hand at him and he turned, walking Romeo down the trail.

Elsa followed the big quarter horse, in no hurry to investigate anything else after the excitement they'd had. Adriana felt the same way.

CHAPTER ELEVEN

Hunter finished his first pass around the staff casitas, main building and guest casitas. He wanted to talk to Mac before he headed up to the garage.

He'd been late getting back with Adriana and then he had to explain the gunshot to Jorge, who met them on the trail, concerned for their welfare. That was pretty smart thinking on his part because there was almost no cell reception out there unless a person wanted to hike to the top of the ravine.

Now, he wanted to know what Mac had found. He strode across the fork in the dirt road and stood near the barn. He flashed the light from his phone a couple times and waited.

The door of the stable manager's office closed behind him and he spun around.

Mac walked toward him. "So now you're chasing mountain lions, too?"

He shook his head. "That was a little closer than I would have liked, but I'm glad everyone is aware. As long as he has plenty of rabbits and coyotes, we should be safe, but Jorge agreed we should keep the doors to the barn closed at night."

"Ah, I was wondering why they were shut." She glanced at the large barn doors before returning her gaze to him. "So I'm guessing you want to know what I found."

He nodded. After this afternoon, he was glad he'd let Mac take over the investigation of the swingers forum. He probably would have thrown his laptop out the window halfway through it. He understood Adriana loved sex and had slept with a lot of people, but now that they had made love, though she was still fighting it, he didn't want to know what people thought of her.

He still struggled with what it was they did have. It was more than just sex.

"I'll tell you this, you don't ever want to read those." Mac shook her head. "What some people wrote about Adriana had my blood boiling. I think you'd be ready to kill."

He didn't deny his interest in Adriana. How could he when Mac had seen him sucking on Adriana's neck the first time he'd kissed her and knew he'd been on the trail with her? "Were you able to find anyone who might hold a grudge against her?"

"There were a few posters that stood out. There was Dds4love, but I highly doubt it's your Dom. The tone is like a woman whining or pouting."

"That would be the sub. She was upset, but I don't think she's the type to do anything beyond complain unless her Dom tells her to, which he very well could."

"Okay. The second one was PattiCake who is obviously the little blonde from the foursome. She posts every night, really late. Either she's posting about what they are doing, have done, or what she'd like to do and Adriana is definitely someone she'd like to do."

"I've been wondering about her. I'll cross reference her with the guest list and locations. You said there was a third person speaking about Adriana?"

Mac laughed. "No, I said there were a few who stood out. There were over two hundred people talking about Adriana, but from what I read, it was only a couple dozen who'd actually slept with her."

Hunter fisted his hands to control the anger that built fast. It was stupid, but he couldn't help it. "So the third person is?"

"The third is Stud21." She rolled her eyes. "I actually tracked names up to Stud153. Talk about not being creative or having big egos. Stud21 is pretty impressed with himself, but it sounds like Adriana wasn't and didn't accept his invitation. His posts are a bit like a stalker's."

"In what way?"

"He writes about what Adriana wore. When she went to the stock room. What time she closed the bar. He even mentioned what she had for lunch."

Hunter opened his mouth, but Mac held up her hand.

"And yes, he has been here when the judge was here."

He didn't like the sound of that. "Has he been here this week?"

Mac nodded.

"Great, Stud21 doesn't give me a lot to go on."

"No, but we know he's a swinger, and I can tell you from his posts, he's married."

Hunter relaxed. "That does help. We don't get a lot of swingers. As soon as I'm off shift, I'll cross reference those with what I've found and I should be able to track down who it is. Then I can gather the evidence I need to help Adriana press charges. Thank you."

"Glad I could help." Mac started to leave, but Hunter grasped her arm.

She broke through his grip and turned around, foot flying toward his groin.

He pulled his hips back just in time. "Shit, Mac, I wasn't attacking you."

She grimaced. "Sorry. Just instinct."

That was a shit more than instinct, but he wasn't going to ask. "If you ever need my help, all you have to do is ask."

"Good to know." She gave him a nod before heading toward the Old West town.

He'd been skeptical when Kendra had hired Mac, but she'd just proved she was a good team player, not to mention physically able.

He strode back to the fork in the road to head for the garage. His mind whirred with possibilities. He was anxious to figure out who Stud21 was and find a photo of him. He would also check the guest casita lights from above and keep a closer eye on the foursome. And just to be sure he left no stone unturned, he'd cross reference all three in the Dom-Dom-sub relationship.

There was a new urgency in his investigations. At first, using his old skills had made him feel awake again, but now his gut said if he didn't figure out who was behind all this, Adriana would be gone either because Kendra couldn't afford to keep her around or more likely, Adriana would simply leave.

It had taken all he had to pretend he couldn't see she was almost completely packed. The fact was, he didn't want her to go.

~~~~~

Adriana reluctantly opened her eyes at the noise coming from her front door. "It figures."

Throwing the covers off her nude body, she padded through the living room in her bare feet. Whoever was pounding on her door deserved to find her naked. She'd been having the best dream with Hunter, a sex swing, and nipple clips.

She pulled the door open fast. "What?"

Lacey stilled, her fist in midair. "We need to talk."

She squinted at the sunlight streaming in behind Lacey. "What time is it?"

Lacey brushed by her. "It's eleven. Now can you please throw something on? This is an emergency."

Adriana closed the door. "Fine, fine. Only for you." She walked into her bedroom and pulled a red silk robe off a hanger. She'd been thinking of giving it away, which is why it had escaped a box.

Tying it, she strode into the living room and headed straight to the kitchen. "Okay, talk while I make coffee."

Lacey sat on one of the kitchen counter chairs. "I was balancing your checkbook."

She measured out the coffee and dumped it in the maker. "Is it that time of the month already?"

"Yes, and there are some major discrepancies."

Her stomach contracted. Crap, had she overdrawn again? She filled the coffeepot with water and poured it in. "Okay, give it to me straight. How much?"

"Around three thousand seven hundred and fifty dollars."

She spun around and faced her friend. "There's no fucking

way I spent that much. Someone must have hacked my account." Great, just what she needed now.

Lacey shook her head. "No, you're not overdrawn. That's how much more money is in your account versus what you wrote in your checkbook."

"What? How?" She leaned against the counter, wishing the coffee was ready because her brain was definitely not working.

"That's what I came here to find out. Where did the extra money come from?"

"I haven't a clue. This makes no sense. When did this money appear?" Had she rubbed some old lamp and had her secret wish granted? No, any genie smart enough to grant wishes would have given her a thousand men, not a thousand dollars.

She pushed away the image of Hunter that flashed through her head.

Lacey pulled out a slip of paper with her neat handwriting. "They appeared on two different days this week. The first day had two deposits and the second had three. Two of the deposits were for over a thousand dollars each."

The coffeemaker beeped it was ready and Adriana poured herself a cup. Taking a sip, she tried to make her brain work. She leaned back against the sink and faced Lacey. "Who would *deposit* money into my account? It's not like I've been having sex for pay. Wouldn't someone steal the money, not give it to me?"

Lacey's brows lowered in worry. "I bet it was that photo site Kendra told me about."

Beyond pissed off, she slammed her coffee mug down on the counter, sloshing hot coffee over her hand, but she didn't care. "Fuckin-a! I didn't set that up, so how could I get the money from it?"

Lacey's eyes widened. "What if someone had your bank account number?"

That Lacey believed her lowered her anger back down to a simmer. "Now how could someone—" Lacey's knowing look had her thinking. "Crap, my car. That's why they broke into my car, to get my bank account number. They didn't have to take anything. All they needed was to snap a photo and move on."

Lacey looked like she was about to cry. "Kendra is going to hear of this eventually, even if I don't tell her."

Hell, her prospects looked so bleak, she didn't think it mattered. "No, go ahead and tell her. I don't want you to lose your job, too. Last Chance Ranch needs your income as well as Cole's. I can't put myself before all those horses you save."

Lacey stood and came into the kitchen, her intention obvious. She wanted to give her a hug.

Adriana put her hands out in front of her. "No, I can't deal with a hug right now. Just go back to work. I'll figure this out."

Lacey eyes revealed her hurt, but she nodded and stepped back. "Let me know if you discover anything."

She snorted. "Yeah, will do."

Lacey gave her one last sympathetic look and left.

"Fuck." She lowered her head to the kitchen counter and closed her eyes. What had she done to deserve this? Who the hell was messing with her life? If she got her hands on them—

Adriana snapped her head up. "No more vacation." Stalking into her bedroom, she pulled open the top drawer of her nightstand and pulled out her 357 Magnum. From now on, this baby would be with her no matter where she went. She was done being the victim.

An image of her mother's unemotional eyes made her pause.

The day her father was shot, the coyotes had taken her mother into the bedroom and raped her. As a child, she had no idea what they were doing, but her mother's screams had kept her from finding out. However, they had motivated her to crawl out of her hiding place and across the bloody floor to her father's body and pull his cell phone from his belt. Even then she knew the coyotes were bad men.

The lady's voice on the other end of the phone when she called 9-1-1 had calmed her down. She'd crawled back into the cabinet that was supposed to contain an entertainment center, but they didn't have one. She stayed there until the police arrived, the lady on the phone talking to her the whole time.

Nope, she was no one's victim. Adding bullets to the gun, she rested it on the bed and dressed in a pair of jeans, tank top, and long sleeve button down. She tucked the gun into the back of her jeans, underneath the shirt.

Right now, she had no idea who was after her, but things could get pretty sticky, especially for Poker Flat. She stilled. The place had felt like home, probably because she'd been given one when she was hired.

Kendra had built the staff casitas because the resort was out in the middle of nowhere, the closest town fifteen miles away. Adriana didn't want something to happen to Poker Flat just because someone had it out for her. She could move on to something else, somewhere else. But first she needed to make sure whoever was after her knew she was leaving.

There was one place she could go to be sure everyone in a thirty-mile radius knew. It was the biggest gossip spot in the area and they served great pizza too. After tying on a pair of strappy high heels, she grabbed her keys. Going to the Black Mustang bar would kill two birds with one stone. She could tell people she was leaving Poker Flat tomorrow for good and she could find a sex partner for her last night in town.

Her throat closed when she imagined Hunter's reaction. He'd be pissed and probably go back to not saying anything to anyone. And his nightmares…

She swallowed hard and strode out her door. The man had done just fine before they'd had sex. He was a big boy. He'd live.

She caught a ride up to the garage with Andrew who was his usual polite self. Walking the resort in cowboy boots was one thing. Trying to do it in high heels was plain stupid.

"Thank you, Andy." She kissed him on the cheek as he stopped the golf cart at the entrance to the garage. "If you want, when you get off work, come join me for pizza. I'll be at the Black Mustang."

He blushed as he tipped his hat. "Thank you."

She laughed as she made her way to her car and got in. She'd bet a hundred dollars Andy didn't show up. He was one of the good ones, except he worked at Poker Flat. Hmm, now that was a puzzle.

Pulling out of the garage, she turned her Camaro onto the dirt road. She had to keep the top up or all her papers and receipts would blow out, but what did that matter? She planned to leave anyway. As much as she would have enjoyed the feel of the wind in her hair, littering wasn't her thing.

When she arrived at the bar, she found a parking space right in front of the horse trough. It was all for show, the building being less than twenty years old, but it was part of the atmosphere.

She'd had enough of cowboys for a while, but bikers, construction workers, landscapers, even other bartenders hung out at the Black Mustang. As she stepped out of the car, a cat call came from behind her and she turned and waved.

Now that put a smile on her face. Stepping inside, she scanned the room out of habit, immediately sizing up the possibilities. Three men played pool, four sat at the bar and two tables held a mix of men and women, but it was early yet.

She took a seat at the bar. "Hey, Cutter, I'll take a beer."

The man behind the bar grinned. "Haven't seen you here in a while, Adriana. What've you been up to?"

While he poured her usual from the tap, she watched. "The typical stuff, sex, work, sex, sleep. Did I mention sex?"

He slapped a coaster down on the bar and plopped her mug on it. "No wonder we haven't seen you."

"Yeah." She gave him a pout. "And you won't be seeing me again. I'm moving on."

Cutter tugged at the earring in his right ear. "Don't that suck. Where you headed?"

She shrugged as she sipped the cold beer. The CO_2 was off. Too much head on it. "I was thinking Southern California. I hear they have some great beach bars down there and everyone is in perfect shape."

The bartender gave her a disgusted look. "Yeah, because it's all fake."

She laughed. "So you don't think I'll fit in?"

He shook his head. "Not a chance. You should stay here."

Another customer waved him over, and Cutter moved down the bar. She took another sip of beer. The man sitting one stool to the left of her turned. "You're leaving town?"

She grinned. This was going to work beautifully.

~~~~~

Adriana stared at the shot of whiskey. She should have shut herself off three shots ago. Okay, eight shots ago, but Cutter was too busy chatting with his buds over the basketball game on television to notice the only way she was getting off her stool was to fall off.

Crap, just two weeks ago after a threesome of hunky males, she'd thought her life was as perfect as it could get. This week, it hit the skids and fell right over the cliff down into hell. What the fuck happened?

The Dom started her bad luck streak. It was all his fault. The crowning glory wasn't the money. No, now she had more money to start her new life. The icing on the shit cake was Hunter. The man had spoiled her favorite part of life—sex.

Despite trying to get her body interested in almost every man, and a few women, who had walked into the bar in the last five hours, she felt nothing. She even let a guy feel up her ass while she shot pool and still, not even a twinge of excitement.

Hunter was a jerk for doing this to her. Her one pleasure in life. She picked up the shot, threw it back and plunked the shot glass back down on the bar. There was always alcohol. Maybe now her body might be interested.

She looked at the man sitting next to her. He wore a fire department t-shirt and his bulky arms were definitely drool-worthy. Maybe he knew Cole. She gave his body a complete inspection as he cheered for his team.

Nope, not even his tight ass did anything. She was so *not* screwed.

The bar door opened and a man came in wearing a black

cowboy hat and black tee. Her body came alive within seconds until she saw the blue jeans, which had her glancing at his bearded face. All physical attraction fizzled. Fuck.

This was torture. She needed to go home to bed, but there was no way she could drive. She could probably coax any one of these hunks to drive her home in exchange for a little sex, but in her condition, she wouldn't even be able to fake it.

She stuck her hand in her back pocket for her cellphone before remembering Kendra still had it. "Hey, Cutter, can I borrow your phone?"

He glanced her way. "Sure." He looked back at the game then strode over. "Here you go. Did you want another shot?"

She grinned. "Of course."

He handed her his phone then did a quick pour before returning to the game.

Crap, without her phone she didn't have her numbers. There was no way she'd call the resort. Kendra or Wade would answer. She tried to get her brain to function. Whose number did she know?

Lacey.

Hah, she'd call Lacey. She glanced at the time on the phone. It was just after nine, Lacey would still be awake. It took her two tries, but she finally dialed the right number combination onto the screen.

"Hey, Lacey. Think you could give me a ride back to Poker Flat?"

"Adriana, is that you?"

"Of course it's me. Who'd you think it was? Never mind. I need a ride. I'm drunk."

"I can hear that. Where are you?" Lacey's voice sounded way too concerned.

"The Black Mustang. They have great pizza here." She did have pizza earlier and it *was* good. At least she thought it was.

"Okay, just sit tight."

"Now that I can do. Don't think I could get off this stool anyway." She chuckled. It just seemed funny.

Lacey said goodbye and hung up.

Adriana stared at the phone a few minutes. She couldn't remember if she was supposed to do something else. Shrugging, she put the phone on the bar and threw back the shot.

"Hey, Cutter, thanks for the phone."

He nodded absently, but didn't come over.

Oh well, so much for getting another shot. She eyed the firefighter guy again. Maybe he could bring her to Cole's and then Lacey wouldn't have to drive so far. No, that didn't make sense.

When a commercial break came on, Cutter came back to retrieve his phone. "Do you need anything else?"

She eyed him speculatively. She'd always thought he was hot, so why not tonight? "Hmm, how about another shot and a kiss."

Cutter smirked. "I think I can manage that." Leaning over the bar, he wrapped his hand around her neck and pulled her toward him for a kiss.

Now maybe she'd feel something. Just as her lips were about to touch his, the shot glass flew across the bar and fell on the floor behind it.

"Ah shit." Cutter let her go. "Hold that thought."

As he cleaned up the mess, she twirled around on the stool and studied the rest of the bar. It was hopeless. There was no one of any interest. What the fuck would she do with the rest of her life? Sex made life worth living.

Cutter gave a sigh. "Okay, that's all set."

She twirled back around to face him but missed stopping and found herself looking at the rest of the place again. She laughed. "That didn't work. Let me try again." She pushed off against the stool's legs and spun full circle again.

Maybe there were other fun things to do. She spun again, but this time Cutter reached across the bar and stopped her by grabbing the back of the stool. She stopped but her world kept spinning.

"Oh crap, I think I'm going to be sick."

Cutter stepped back. "If you are, you better hit the ladies room or go outside." He beat a hasty retreat.

Adriana held fast to the bar, taking deep breaths, trying to keep her stomach from coming up. She'd never been so drunk she'd vomited and she certainly didn't plan to now. She stared at the cash register across from her and counted to one hundred.

Finally, her stomach calmed. She could order another shot, but that probably wasn't a good idea. Maybe she should get some fresh air. She carefully swiveled around to face the door. She was trying to decide how to climb down from her stool when the door opened and another cowboy walked in.

He looked just like Hunter and her body responded. Finally.

The cowboy stalked toward her.

Crap, it *was* Hunter. "What are you doing here? Aren't you working?"

He frowned at her. "Lacey said you needed a ride, but I saw your car parked outside."

"That Benedict Arnie, *she* was supposed to get me so no one would know."

His frown turned into a scowl. "Are you drunk?"

She rolled her eyes, but they stuck halfway around and she blinked. "Duh. That's why I called for a ride."

His mouth formed a straight line and his jaw became rigid. The little tic in his cheek she'd noticed when they had sex against her casita wall was back. Maybe he was turned on. Wanted to take advantage of her. She was all for that.

"Let's go." He grabbed hold of her hand and pulled her off the chair.

She stumbled, her high heels wobbling before she started to go down.

Hunter scooped her up in his arms before she hit. Crap, the guy's reflexes were fast. She leaned her head back to yell at Cutter. "I'll be back tomorrow to settle up."

He nodded absently, his attention on the game.

Hunter took her outside and leaned her against a truck.

"Hmm, is this yours?" She held on to the truck bed to keep upright.

He backed away from her as if he couldn't stand to touch her.

What the hell did she do? He's the one who ruined sex for her.

Then he bent down and untied her strappy heels. She stepped onto the cool asphalt. "Oh that's so much better."

He silently threw the shoes in the backseat, but he made no move to open the door for her. Wasn't a cowboy supposed to do that? She looked at the handle. Could she make it over there without falling?

"What the fuck were you doing?" The cold tone of Hunter's voice permeated her confusion.

She grinned. "What's it look like I was doing? I was getting drunk."

His jaw became more rigid, if that was possible. Could he actually speak with it locked like that? She just had to find out. "You ruined me." She let go with one hand to point at the bar, but started to fall, so she grabbed on to the truck again. "Not one man or woman in there appealed to me. Sex was my life. Thanks to you, my interest in it is gone."

Hunter took a menacing step toward her, crowding her against the truck, causing her knees to wobble. He didn't say a word, but her whole body turned on, way on. She wanted him to take her right there on the ground. It was like he'd flipped a switch and every sexual impulse in her lit up.

He stood there, his jaw tight, her heart racing.

Then he turned away, fisting his hands. "You're not worth it."

His words were like a jug of cold water poured over her head. "You just figured that out?"

He didn't look at her, but she felt the rage coming off him in waves and the image of him strangling the Dom with the whip had her anger changing to fear. This was the Hunter she'd depended on to protect her and now she was the bad guy, the enemy in his mind. Freak, she was in trouble.

She looked past his back to the door of the bar. Would they hear her screams? Would she have the chance to scream? Maybe now was a good time.

Hunter finally turned around and looked at her. His eyes glittered in the parking lot lights like moonlight off steel. "You could have killed someone."

His voice was raspy as if he fought to stay in control.

She wanted to argue, but her instinct told her she needed to calm him down if she wanted to make it out of this alive. She lowered her head. "I know. That's why I called for a ride."

He didn't acknowledge her statement. "Killed someone innocent. Someone anxious to see me."

Huh? Her brain was too fuzzy to make sense. What was he talking about?

One of his fisted hands came up, but his gaze was past her. "Eighteen months. We were apart eighteen months and thirty-two minutes before we saw each other again, and he hit her with his semi. That drunk crushed her."

Adriana's heart cracked as tears filled her eyes. His anguish flowed over her. She wanted to comfort him, but he was pissed at her. Why was he pissed at her again?

"I couldn't let her go." His fist came down. "She was my light. All that was good. All that I destroyed by going over for a second tour. I was an idiot."

"No." She shook her head. The blame was the drunk driver's, not his.

His gaze moved to her face at her voice. "I sold everything to keep her alive. I needed her. But she wanted to go and I let her."

She couldn't stand there and see him hurt so much. She took a shaky step forward. The ground spun, causing her to lose her balance.

He caught her once again just as her stomach decided it had enough. Instead of dropping her, he kept her steady while she heaved the alcohol that incapacitated her.

Finally, there was nothing left. She straightened, her stomach and throat sore. "I'm sorry." For so many things. For his wife, his heartbreak, for getting involved with him. He was used to an angel, not someone like her.

Hunter didn't say anything. He simply walked her to the front door of the truck and helped her inside. He jumped into the driver seat and leaned over to open the glove compartment. Pulling out tiny box of tissues, he handed it to her.

She took it, murmuring a thank you, and wiped her mouth. Didn't she feel like dog poop now, both inside and out?

Hunter started the truck and headed back to Poker Flat. He didn't say a single word the whole way.

It gave her a lot of time to think. Her idea of taking off to California now looked like the only solution. Once she was gone, Poker Flat would be safe and Hunter could move on to a better woman.

She'd ignored the feelings she had developed for him, but tonight showed her exactly how much he meant to her. She'd never wanted to help someone so much, especially a man. It looked like her days of meaningless sex were over.

Luckily, he didn't know her well enough to like her too much. Even though he now "knew" her in the Biblical sense. She smiled inside.

It was for the best for everyone, except maybe her, but she was tough. She would live. She could handle it better than anyone at Poker Flat.

When they arrived, Mac was waiting with a golf cart. "Hey, you look like shit."

She grinned. "No kidding. You try drinking for five hours then vomiting everything up, and see what you look like."

"Whoa, I better take you home. Hop in."

She glanced back at Hunter, who stood outside in the moonlight. He looked at her, but didn't say anything.

"Thank you."

He made no response. He didn't even move, not even the tic in his cheek.

She turned away and climbed into the golf cart. "I feel like crap."

Mac gave her a nervous look. "Just hold on until I get you home, okay?"

"Okay."

CHAPTER TWELVE

Adriana slammed her trunk closed and breathed a sigh of relief that it didn't pop open. It was hard enough deciding what she needed to take with her and what to send, never mind sneaking around in broad daylight.

She'd hitched a ride with the liquor delivery man. His second stop after Poker Flat was always the Black Mustang, so she was able to retrieve her car and settle up with Cutter. He didn't charge her for at least five shots, so she left him a big tip. Then she closed out her account at the bank. If someone wanted to dump money into her account, she was damn well going to keep it.

Once back at her casita, the fun had begun. Avoiding staff and guests on a busy day had been a challenge, but she'd done it. She could fit one more box on her passenger seat and she'd be ready to leave.

She wouldn't say goodbye to anyone. It was her fault for growing attached. In the bordello, she'd been good at keeping people at a distance because the girls came and went for various reasons. Some found better jobs, others found love, and some, like herself, just decided to move on.

But Poker Flat and the staff had burrowed under her skin. Hunter had... Refusing to think about him because of the ache in her chest, she strode to her golf cart and drove it to the edge of the ravine where the dirt road sloped downward.

She gazed out at the resort as the sunset splashed an orange-pink glow over the buildings. Most everyone was at dinner. She could see a few people around the outside bar. Kendra was serving. That woman had made a cool retreat for those who preferred to be nude.

She wished her huge success.

Adriana remained at the edge of the ravine, watching and waiting. Finally, Mac came out of the barn and walked to the stable manager building. Clear on that front. This would be her last trip to her casita, so she didn't want anyone to see her.

Then movement down by casita number one caught her eyes. Hunter. Even from where she was, she recognized his walk. It was predatory, like the mountain lion he'd scared away.

She swallowed hard at the hitch in her heart. Fuck, this was going to hurt like hell. Just another reason not to say goodbye.

It was now or never. She put the golf cart into motion and drove straight to her casita. She parked it on her patio so it wasn't so noticeable. Of course, Hunter would notice it, but he was so furious, she was confidant she wouldn't hear from him. She told him she wasn't good at the connecting thing. She just wasn't good enough. Her leaving would be better for everyone.

Now all she had to do was wait. Lacey and Andrew had already left. She'd never see them again. Her plan was to leave after Kendra closed the bar. The foursome would walk to their casita and Hunter would keep an eye on them. But he'd see her as she drove up the ravine to the garage. She needed him to be distracted because he was the only thing that could keep her at Poker Flat and it was better she leave, especially for him.

She walked into her casita and kicked off her sneakers, thinking over possible ideas to get Hunter to the other side of the resort. Once she figured out what to do, all she had to do was pack up her food and go. She'd come up with something, but first she'd heat up one last Selma meal that Lacey had dropped by.

Hunter heard splashing in the conversation pool and walked over to be sure there was no glass nearby. The guests were pretty good about that, but after drinking all day, sometimes they forgot.

Three people chatted, the signature Poker Flat plastic glasses on the stone table between them. He nodded as they waved and continued his patrol. He'd totally lost it last night when he found Adriana too drunk to even stand on her own.

He couldn't believe she'd done that. As a bartender, she of all people should know when to stop. What the fuck was wrong with her?

He should also figure out what was wrong with him. He'd thought he'd conquered his aversion to people drinking, but he obviously hadn't.

Maybe he never would.

"Hunter?"

He turned at the sound of his name. Kendra had walked out from behind the bar and caught up with him.

"Do you need something?"

She had on her poker face, which cued him in that it wasn't good news. "I wanted to let you know I'm going to let Adriana go.

Lacey found deposits to her bank account from the days the photo site was up." She raised her hand. "No, I still don't think she did it, but what else is going to happen? I can't risk the whole resort. If she figures out who is doing this to her and takes care of it, then I'll be happy to hire her back."

He wanted to argue with her, but he didn't blame her.

"I just wanted you to know, so you can decide what you want to do."

He'd forgotten he'd told her he'd quit too. Adriana was going to be— Wait a minute. "How big were the deposits made to Adriana's account?"

Kendra sighed. "Some were over a thousand dollars." She glanced back at the bar and noticed a guest waiting. "We can talk more about this tomorrow."

He gave her a quick nod as his mind raced. One of the guests was the regional manager for a bank and he was sure there was a bank in the office complex where the site had been created. The question was, was it Adriana's bank?

Anyone could deposit money into her account, but if it was someone who worked at her bank, they could ask one of the tellers to come to their office and give the employee the deposit to make. There'd be no video footage of them giving the teller the cash, only of the teller making the deposit. It was more likely someone who worked at a bank would think of doing that than someone who owned a landscaping business, which one of the suspects did.

Heading for the fork in the road, he waved Mac down as she walked across the dirt area in front of the barn.

"What's up?"

"I need a few minutes to check something. I think I might

have a lead on who has been making Adriana look bad. Do you mind watching the resort while I take a half hour to work on it?"

"No, go. I've got this."

He nodded and headed straight for his casita. He was pretty sure it was either Patti from the foursome or Tina from the Dom-Dom-sub relationship who worked at a bank. If it was, they could finally confront her.

Once home, he turned on the laptop and grabbed a water. Pulling up the spread sheet, he glanced across the three highlighted lines. Stud21 was a restaurant owner. Patti was a real estate agent. Tina was a regional manager for a bank.

He pulled up the list of companies in the office complex. There it was. Triumph whipped through him. "I've got you now."

He didn't know which bank Adriana had. He'd ask her after his shift. But just to be sure, he scanned down the occupations of all the guests who had been at the resort while the judge was.

Tina was the only banker. To be thorough, he double checked the two Doms, John and Gary. John owned a financial advisement firm. That could be where Tina obtained the money from. He may have told her to do it.

Yes! He had motive, means, and opportunity. But he couldn't jump to conclusions. He had to confirm Adriana's bank was the one in the complex.

Closing the laptop, he headed directly for the bar. Kendra was slammed with people so he strode down around the guest casitas. When he came back up, she was still busy so he walked through the main building then jogged up to the garage. He walked between the vehicles and noticed the red SUV wasn't there anymore.

But the memory of it triggered the image of him and his wife buying it together so she'd be safe. Little had they known, nothing could withstand the impact of a semi-truck.

He stilled, waiting for the familiar anger to come to the surface, but it didn't make it that far. Instead, sadness overwhelmed his anger. He wasn't sure if it was better. It certainly didn't feel better. He continued his patrol. As he walked by the staff cars, he noticed Adriana had her car back. She must have picked it up during the day.

She would be pissed when she found out it was Tina. He pictured her reaction. First, she'd swear. Then she'd slap both hands on her hips and spit. That image alone had him smiling and the sadness took a back seat.

He took out his flashlight and looked in her car. Damn, she had boxes in the back seat on top of all her paperwork. He couldn't see any of it. He flashed his light over the front seat, but there were no bank receipts there.

How could she pack her car with a hangover? She had to have had a bad one. His hands clenched as he remembered her inebriated state. When he'd seen her in the bar, he was pissed because she looked so hot, but when he realized she was drunk, it infuriated him. She should never have put herself in that situation. Any one of the men in that bar could have taken advantage of her.

Maybe they had. He stalked out of the garage. He didn't want her having sex with anyone else. She may not understand it yet, but she was his.

As he reached the ravine ledge, he scanned the resort. More lights were on in the guest casitas and from the lights above the outside bar, there were only a handful left there. He headed that way.

~~~~~

Adriana looked at the clock. The bar should be closed by now. It was time. She looked around the casita that had been her home for over a year. It sucked to have to leave. Quietly, she stepped outside and locked the door.

After loading her box of food on the golf cart, she drove to Hunter's casita. She picked the lock but the door wouldn't open. Damn, he'd added a deadbolt. Moving around to the slider, she checked it for a bar. Crap. How was she supposed to create a distraction if she couldn't break in?

There was one other way in. She looked around the patio and found what she needed. She tugged on one of the pavers that served as a border. Yanking it free, she took it to the window in his door and slammed it hard. The glass cracked but didn't give.

How the hell had he broken an entire slider? She tried again, not as worried about the sound carrying. The paver burst through the window. She pulled her sleeve down past her hand and stuck her arm through, quickly undoing the deadbolt. She hated broken glass.

Leaving the door open, she turned a light on in each room, knocked a couple items off the dresser and threw a living room pillow on the floor before she ran out. Jumping into her golf cart, she drove around to Kendra's house, which was at the end of the staff housing and set back quite a way.

She watched for Mac or Hunter to notice something was wrong. It didn't take long before she heard a shout. She took the opportunity to drive to the fork and head down the path to the bridge at the bottom. By the time the golf cart climbed to the top of the ravine and she glanced back, the lights in Hunter's casita were out.

He'd be looking for the culprit, so she needed to hurry. She couldn't bear to see him before she left, or she might not go. Stopping the golf cart outside the garage, she noticed lights heading along the dirt road that led from the highway to the resort. Great, just what she needed, late arriving guests. She carried her box to her car and put it in the passenger seat.

Running around the vehicle, she jumped in and backed out of the garage. She should have turned right, but she couldn't resist taking one last look. She drove her car around the wooden barrier, following the tracks of the golf carts.

She stopped before the edge. Water filled her eyes and she brushed it away with her arm. It had just been a short stop on her road of life. She'd get over it.

As she looked over the staff casitas, a light flicked on in hers. "Hey, I haven't even left yet. Have some respect."

The lights of the guests coming onto the resort shone in her rearview mirror and she shaded her eyes. She'd wait until they turned into the garage then she'd turn around and leave before they left the garage to go down to the resort.

She waited for the vehicle to turn but it didn't. Crap, did they think this was the way to the resort?

She put her car in reverse when she noticed the vehicle swerve around the barrier. Oh, this wasn't good. It was there to keep people from driving over the ledge. She backed around so she could face the car with her headlights and flash them, but no sooner had she turned sideways than the car sped up and broadsided her.

Hunter tried to still the panic in his heart as he rushed

through the three rooms of Adriana's casita. As he walked out the door, Mac grabbed his arm. "Look."

He stilled at the car lights sitting at the edge of the ravine. Adriana would never kill herself, which meant she was taking a last look. He had to get up there. He sprinted to the front of the main building and grabbed a golf cart. He'd just reached the fork when he saw the lights move. "Fuck."

Pressing the pedal to the floor of the golf cart, he sped down to the bridge.

A crash sounded above him and he looked up. "No!"

Adriana's car teetered on the edge of the ravine, the passenger side over the ridge.

He jumped out of the golf cart and ran up the hill. Just as he crested it, he saw another car stop backing up and head forward again toward Adriana. Pulling his gun from his waist, he dropped to one knee and fired.

The car spun. He fired again. Two tires shot out, but it still tried to move forward. It had to be Tina.

With little choice left, he aimed at the windshield and pulled the trigger. The sedan slowed to a stop and he ran for Adriana's car.

As he approached, he could see she was out cold, the vehicle so old there was no airbag. Her driver side window was busted, probably from her head hitting it. He had to control his breathing. Losing control now wouldn't help her.

He stepped closer. He only had one shot at this. He looked at her old fashioned door locks and was relieved to see they were unlocked. Luckily, the impact was to the back door, a large dent in the metal bent outward, leaving a sharp edge. The problem was, she wore her seatbelt.

The yellow car rocked back and forth a foot each way. Pulling his knife from his pocket, he held it in his right hand and with his left, opened the door slowly. The car creaked toward him. He sliced through the seatbelt before the car started to tip the other way.

He grabbed Adriana by her arms and yanked as the vehicle tipped over the ridge, the sharp edge of the bent metal caught the side of his arm and sliced it open. "Argh."

Between the pain in his arm and her weight, he had to throw himself to the ground to avoid being taken over the side. The crash as the car landed shook the ravine and then the night lit up as it exploded.

He rolled them over, protecting her from the heat when the fireball rose up the canyon wall and dissipated into the night air.

"Adriana?" He pressed two fingers against her neck and breathed a sigh of relief. She had a pulse. She was too full of life to die. He sat up and tried to use his right arm to hold her, but it was weak.

"Shit." He was losing too much blood. His knife was five feet away so he crawled over to it and lifted it in his left hand. In no time he'd ripped his shirt open. Fuck, he needed a tourniquet and fast.

No one was going to think they were up there. They would assume Adriana was in the car. He tried to reach his phone but the blood on his hand kept him from gripping it. Darkness threatened his vision. If he passed out, he would bleed to death.

He didn't want to die. For the first time in a long time, he wanted to live.

"Can I help." Adriana's voice surprised him.

He turned to see her crawling toward him. She was alright.

Relief surged through him. "I need you to tie this around my arm, up here really tight."

She looked at his arm and her eyes widened. She shook her head. "I-I c-can't."

The darkness was becoming too hard to resist. "You can. You have to stop the flow of blood. If you don't, I'll die." His voice sounded far away to him. Did he actually say that or did he dream it?

Maybe this was just another one of his nightmares. He hoped so. He could dream he felt better and they were having sex. Yeah, that's what they were doing. And he was convincing her there was more than sex between them, giving it his cowboy's best shot of getting her to admit she felt something stronger.

His gut said she did. His gut was never wrong. To hell with nightmares, this could be a great dream. The darkness reached for him and he slipped into its waiting arms.

Adriana couldn't take her eyes from the blood covering Hunter's arm. It flowed like a tiny river over the "Julie" tattoo, so different from the puddle her father had next to him. "I can get help."

When Hunter didn't respond, fear sliced through her. "Hunter? Hunter!"

She pulled his good arm, but his head just rolled.

"Fuck. Fuck. Fuck. Don't you dare die on me." She looked at the strip of material in his good hand. Even that had blood on it. Freakin-a, she couldn't do this.

She had to do this. He said he would die.

Pain filled her chest at the possibility. She swallowed hard and grasped the strip of material in both hands, trying not to breathe deep as the warm iron smell tried to pull her back to when she was eight. The blood kept flowing down his arm.

She swallowed hard and moved her gaze to where he'd pointed to. There was no blood up there. She could keep her eyes on that. Without looking, she threaded the strip of material under his arm and around. When her hand came around, it was wet with blood.

"Fuck. I hate blood." She forced herself to take shallow breaths and tied the two ends together as tight as she could. The memory of Hunter choking the Dom with the whip helped her ignore the blood all over him. His arm was so large. Was it tight enough?

She forced herself to look below the material. Barely a trickle ran down his arm now. She watched as the tiny thread wiggled its way along his forearm and off his hand to soak into the dry desert ground. She wanted to tighten her knot, but if she loosened it to do that, all the blood would flow again.

Even as she had the thought, her stomach heaved and she leaned away to vomit. When she finished, she looked around. He needed help. There was a car not far away but its windshield was cracked. What the fuck hap—"Oh, crap."

That car had hit her broadside. So where was her car? She looked at the ledge not five feet away and her stomach heaved again.

She wiped her mouth on her sleeve. It didn't take a genius to figure out what had happened. She owed Hunter her life.

Freakin-a. He already had her heart. Now she had to save him.

She started to stand and fell over, the ground moving like it had the night before when she was drunk. She touched her head and found a huge bump. "Ouch."

Note to self: if it hurts, don't touch it.

She crawled back to Hunter. "Okay, you can't die on me." Maybe she could crawl to the golf cart and honk the horn. "Yeah right, over the noise going on down there. They'd never hear it."

If only she had her phone. The sounds of sirens in the distance gave her hope. She took off her long-sleeve shirt and covered Hunter. She'd seen on television where they kept accident victims warm. This wasn't exactly an accident. More like a homicidal maniac event.

She glared at the car yards away. Whoever was in it better not wake up or she and Hunter were sitting ducks. Unless…she reached behind her for her gun. Crap, she'd put it in the glove compartment.

Hunter groaned and she stroked her hand over his short hair. What happened to his cowboy hat? He always wore his hat. She scanned the ground in the moonlight. It bothered her that she couldn't find his hat. Was that wrong?

The sirens grew louder. They must have turned down the dirt road leading to the resort. She watched the desert for a reflection of lights. "Help is on its way. Hold on. Please, hold on."

She blinked back the tears that threatened. There was no way Hunter could die here at Poker Flat. He'd served two tours in Afghanistan, for God's sake. She forced herself to look at the wrap she'd tied. No more blood flowed below it. That was a good thing, right? Or did it mean his whole arm would die?

The reflection of red across the desert floor flooded the area now. They were almost here. The sound became deafening. Freak, why did they leave those on? It wasn't like there was any traffic.

She watched a big-ass fire truck drive around the barrier and head right for the road down to the resort. She waved as the headlights shone on them and the truck came to a sudden stop.

Men jumped out and two headed for the car. To hell with that person. "Over here!" Two large men ran toward her.

"Adriana?"

"Hi, Cole. About time you got here." She gave him a smile, more than happy to see him.

He spoke into his radio. "Dispatch, we need an ambulance."

She nodded. He was a good firefighter and a take-control kind of man, like Hunter. Lacey was very lucky.

He wrapped a blanket around her shoulders. "Can you stand?"

She shook her head then stopped when the ground started to spin again. She reached out, and he caught her arm. "Whoa, there. Just sit while I take a look at…" He glanced down at Hunter. "Shit, Cash, what have you done to yourself?"

"He got cut saving me."

Cole gave her an odd look then took Hunter's pulse. "Who tied the tourniquet?"

"I did. Pretty good for a girl who's afraid of blood, huh? Of course, I did throw up twice." Now why did she tell him that?

"Do you know how long it's been on?"

She tried to think. "Since the crash. No, not that long. I don't know."

"No problem, Adriana. We'll take care of him."

The other man covered Hunter up with a blanket as well. "We need to transport him first."

Cole gave the man a scowl. "Mason, I have an ambulance on the way. I need to check—"

"Who's hurt?" A figure ran in front of the headlights. "Cole, tell me, who's hurt?"

"Lacey, you shouldn't have come."

"Don't give me that—Oh Adriana."

From the look in Lacey's eyes, her bump was bigger. She raised her hand then stopped. If it hurt before it would kill to touch it now. "Hunter's hurt." She pointed to him. Then she glared at Cole. "He better live. If he dies, I'm coming after you with my Smith and, oh crap, that's gone too."

Cole laid a large hand on her shoulder. "He's not going to die."

He spoke into his radio again. "Clark, drive the tanker down below. We'll join you as soon as our patients have been transported."

Adriana looked at Lacey, who had crouched down next to her. "My car is gone."

Lacey didn't say anything. She just opened her arms and gave her a hug.

Adriana hugged her back. She hadn't wanted to leave anyway.

Hunter opened his eyes, immediately recognizing he was in a hospital room. But it was different from the last time. He was in the bed.

He looked at his arm. Shit, it wasn't a dream. Adriana?

He scanned to his left and found her. She was asleep, her head on his leg, her hand clasping his. He'd almost lost her. Another car, another driver, and almost another dead woman. He couldn't let it happen. He would have gone over the edge with her, trying to save her.

She had a bandage wrapped around her head and over her

tangled hair. Shit, she was so beautiful to him. He had to convince her she was his. He squeezed her hand.

"Huh?" She lifted her head, looked at him with her warm brown eyes and blinked. "Hunter?"

"Good morning." He smiled, too happy to have her next to him not to.

She straightened up. "Hunter McKade. You had me worried. How dare you stay unconscious for so long?"

"I'm sorry. If I'd known you were waiting for me to wake up, I promise you I would have woken much sooner."

"You scared me." Her voice was barely a whisper.

"You scared me." He took a deep breath. "Do you know how close you were to going over that ledge with your car?"

She shook her head then held her hand against the good side of her head. "I shouldn't do that. It makes me dizzy. Who was it who hit my car? I couldn't believe that guest ran right into me."

He tried to stay calm, but it was useless. "It wasn't a new guest, it was the Dom's sub, Tina. She was the one who has been making your life hell."

"How would you know? You've been unconscious."

He squeezed her hand in his, still adjusting to the fact that he'd been there, saved her. "Investigative work. Lacey and Mac helped too."

She looked at him like he was crazy. "Meek little Tina?"

"Not so meek. I believe she was the regional manager of your bank. Mac discovered on a forum that she blamed you for her Dom not being allowed at any nudist resorts for miles around." His anger started to build. "She decided you needed to be taught a lesson."

"That bitch." Adriana's hand found her hip, just as he predicted.

His smile broke through his tension. "But she didn't count on Kendra being so loyal to you, so when she didn't fire you time after time, she must have come back to the resort to make you pay." He hesitated over the question he had to ask.

"What is it?"

"I shot her to keep her from ramming you again." He took a deep breath. Killing the enemy, even female enemies in a foreign country was different than this. "I may have killed her."

Adriana's hand came to his chest. "I did see them take someone out of that car and put her in an ambulance. But I haven't heard anything."

"I didn't want to kill her. She probably needed psychological help."

"You think?" Adriana's look had him smiling.

Shit, she'd forced him to face life again and he was so glad he did. He leaned forward, unable to resist her lips a moment longer. Fuck, he'd almost lost her.

Despite the pain in his arm, he brushed her lips with his, the touch calming him.

Adriana's hand wrapped around his neck while she deepened the kiss.

"Whoa, can't you two wait until you're discharged?" Cole walked into the room with Lacey right behind him. She ran straight to Adriana and gave her a hug.

Adriana released his hand to hug her friend back.

Cole shook his head at them. "Good to see you awake, Cash."

Adriana disengaged herself from Lacey's arms. "Hey, Cash doesn't fit him. He's not wearing any black."

He picked at the hospital gown he wore. "No, I believe they call this baby butt blue."

They chuckled at his comment.

"Sorry, black or not, you're still Cash to me." Cole gave a hard nod, like he'd settled that.

"He's a hero to me." Adriana grabbed his hand again, a very good sign as far as he was concerned. "But he wants to know what happened to Tina. Did he kill her?"

Cole stared at him. "How did you know the woman's name was Tina?"

Lacey smiled. "Because he did some of his own detective work and figured out which guest was out to get Adriana." She looked at him. "But how did you know she would try to kill Adriana?"

"I didn't." He looked expectantly at Cole.

The man smirked. "No, you didn't kill her, but your bullet did catch her in the forehead on its way by. She would have kept coming but blood from the wound dripped in front of her eyes and she fainted. That's what she told the EMT when she came to in the ambulance."

"I understand that feeling." Adriana looked at his bandaged arm.

He squeezed her hand to reassure her he was fine. "What was she doing at Poker Flat? Everything up to that point she'd accomplished from off-site. Why show up then?"

Lacey leaned against his bed next to Adriana. "She'd heard on the forums that Adriana was going to leave. I guess she didn't like that at all. She wanted her fired." Lacey looked at her friend. "From the whip they found in her car, we think she planned to punish you, but when she saw your yellow Camaro so close to the edge, she couldn't resist the opportunity to get rid of you once and for all."

Adriana grimaced. "So I was at the right place at the right time to trigger a nut cake."

Lacey shrugged. "I think that's all there is to it."

Cole came around the bed and took Lacey's hand. "But don't worry about her. From what I understand, she'll be under the state's care for a while. She was raving that you had hurt her Dom and you should never have challenged him, and how his reputation was in the mud thanks to you. It didn't make any sense. Detective Anderson said she is facing attempted murder charges and if she doesn't go to jail, she'll still go away for a long time for psychiatric help."

"I'm so glad that's over. Now maybe we can get back to business as usual." Lacey embraced Adriana in another hug and he kept his lips from twitching upward as she rolled her eyes.

Lacey finally let go. "Kendra said as soon as you are feeling better, she wants you back at the bar. She hated having to choose between you and the resort and is thrilled that this is all over."

"I never would have let the resort suffer."

Lacey's eyes teared-up. "I know. You were going to leave without saying goodbye, weren't you?"

Adriana pulled Lacey into her arms and Hunter raised his brow, but she ignored him.

"I was. I didn't want all the tears. Now we don't have to cry." She let Lacey go.

The bookkeeper nodded then leaned over and kissed him on the cheek. "Get better soon, Hunter. We need you back at Poker Flat."

He nodded. "I plan to."

When the couple exited, he gave his full attention to Adriana, who looked completely deflated. That was not a look he liked to see on her. "What is it?

"So once again, I brought it on myself by not being careful in my bedmates."

He released her hand and gently grabbed her chin. "No, you didn't bring this on yourself. The Dom's actions were under his control, not yours. And Tina's actions were her own decision. You did nothing wrong."

She captured his hand, moved it to her lips and kissed it. "Actually, I did. I let you get too close. No other man or woman interests me anymore. I want you to know that you are going to have to meet my sexual needs now because you've spoiled me."

Hunter's soul rejoiced at her words. "I think I'm up for that."

She lowered her brows. "You think?"

He released her hand and cupped her neck, bringing her within an inch of his lips. "I am if you're up for having a relationship."

She gazed into his eyes. "I don't think I have a choice. My heart and body only want you."

He grinned. "Good."

Before she could respond, he kissed her, putting all of his heart into it.

When he released her, she winked. "I think I'm going to like this relationship thing."

Epilogue

Adriana walked around the debris that had been her car. Everything was black. She couldn't see an inch of yellow anywhere.

Good thing she packed only the important stuff in her car and planned to send for the items that were still in boxes in her living room. Hell, wouldn't want to have anything of any value left to pick up the pieces of her life with. She smirked, stifling the groan that wanted to emerge. Even the money she'd taken from her account had been in her purse and her gun was probably melted to the car. So much for catching a break.

She looked up to the top of the ravine wall. She'd never thought of it as that far up, since the winding dirt road made it a gradual climb, but as far as direct height, it was up there.

She returned her gaze to her car and shivered. That could have been her. *Note to self: redefine "catching a break."* She definitely had. She was alive.

A strong arm came around her from behind and she smiled. "It's a good thing I would recognize your scent anywhere, Hunter, or you could have been seriously hurt right now." She turned in his arm to find a smile on his face. He did a lot more of that since getting out of the hospital.

He pulled her against him. "What are you doing here? I woke up and you were gone."

She shrugged. "I guess I just needed to see for myself that nothing was salvageable."

"It doesn't matter. I have the only thing of any importance."

"Good point." She grinned before giving him a passionate kiss. When he broke away, she found herself itching to ditch her clothes. She was still on sick leave because of her head, so she technically didn't have to wear her clothes. Good thing because they were all burned.

She stepped away and looked at the mess that was her life. Her old life. Now she would begin a new one and see where it led her. "I guess I'll start by buying new clothes."

Hunter stepped in front of her. "But you still have boxes in your apartment that are overflowing. Don't you have clothes in there?"

She thought back to what was in those boxes and gave him a seductive smile. "Oh there are clothes in there. I have at least six different body stockings, five corsets, eighteen costumes, eleven teddies in different styles, some—"

Her gaze was caught by a shiny object on the ground not five feet away. Releasing Hunter's hand, she scrambled over the rocks and debris and picked it up. It was Lady's rabies tag. Closing her hand over it, her eyes misted.

"What did you find?"

She made her way back to him and showed him. "It's Lady's tag."

He cupped her chin with his hand. "You really loved her, didn't you?"

She nodded, not willing to give in to the tears. They weren't just for Lady. Her whole life had been turned upside down because of one unbalanced person.

Hunter brushed away a tear that fell down her cheek.

"Crap, I hate crying. Makes my eyes look like hell later."

He chuckled and wrapped his good arm around her waist. "I spoke to my sister today."

"You did?" He only spoke to his family once a month. "Did you tell them where you're living?"

He shook his head. "No, not yet. They mean well, but I'm not ready for that. But I plan to talk to them once a week until I am."

"Did you tell your sister about your injury and how you were a hero and saved me?" She loved teasing him about that because the man was so humble.

"As a matter of fact, I didn't. I didn't want her worrying about me any more than she already does. But I did tell her about you."

"You did?" This couldn't be good.

He nodded, a secret smile on his face that had her suspicious. "I told her what a great person you were and that your dog died."

She frowned. "That was years ago." She looked at the tag in her hand and slipped it into the back pocket of her shorts.

Hunter grinned. "I know, but she didn't need to know that. I only mentioned it because she told me her dog just had a litter of puppies."

"Puppies?" Her heart constricted as she imagined little Lady when she was just a baby.

"But my sister's dog is a full-blooded Labrador and they think the father is a golden retriever so the puppies will grow into big dogs. Still, I asked her if you could have one."

Freakin-a! A puppy! She wanted to jump up and down, but then she cringed. "Did she say I could?"

"Of course she said yes." He shook his head. "The minute I told her my girlfriend might be interested, she was more than happy to part with one."

Girlfriend? Holy crap, she was a girlfriend now. Her life was changing faster than a rattlesnake could strike.

Hunter raised his brows. "So? Do you want one?"

"Duh. I'd love one." She wrapped her arm around his neck and gave him a thank-you kiss. She'd begun to understand there were all kinds of kisses to be given and received.

When she let him go, he took her hand and led her from the scene. They were halfway across the bridge over the creek when he stopped. "I have a proposition for you."

"I like propositions." She wiggled her eyebrows.

"Good." He leaned back against the bridge railing and pulled her toward him. "Since most of your belongings are toast—"

"Really?" She raised her brows that he could use such a pun.

He chuckled, a sound she was growing incredibly fond of. "Sorry. Let me rephrase. Since your belongings are gone and what you have left is already packed up, how about you move into my casita with me."

She froze. Live with a man. She'd never done that before. "I don't know how."

He laughed. "All the better."

"I can cook, but that's about it. I'm not neat and I leave clothes and sex toys and dirty plates all over the place."

He squeezed her waist where his hand rested. "And I probably have a dozen habits that will drive you crazy, but I think it would be fun to try. I will get to see your smile in the evening and hear your laugh. I love your laugh and your honesty and backbone, too. The fact is, I love you and I want to go through day-to-day life with you."

Her heart leapt at his words.

He smirked. "Besides, we will really get to know each other—in more than the Biblical sense."

Thrilled yet afraid, she looked down at his injured right arm. She may be scared, but her heart wanted this. To know everything she could about him and make sure he knew all there was to know about her. She wouldn't pretend to be something she wasn't.

Her gaze fell on the tattoo on his arm. "Julie." She moved her finger over it. "You know I can't be like your late wife." She looked up into his eyes. What would he think? "Not only do I know nothing about ranching, but I'm pretty sure I'm nothing like her."

Deep sadness filled his gaze before he slowly shook his head. "I wouldn't want you to be. I can't be the husband I used to be. I'm different. I've changed."

She understood what he meant. She had changed too. She'd let people into her heart though she'd refused to accept that and she had a home with friends and a man who loved her. She was a different person now. Not better, just different.

She nodded. "I'd like to try that."

His smile was wide and filled with happiness.

Her heart soared with the knowledge that she'd caused it. She wrapped her arms around him. "Let's go."

He winked. "Your place or mine?"

She laughed. "Ours."

~*The End*~

Read on for an excerpt from Trace's Trouble (Last Chance #2) (http://www.lexipostbooks.com/traces-trouble/)

Chapter One

"Stop right there unless you'd like your head blown off."

At the husky voice, Trace froze, bringing Lightyear to a halt as his gaze swung to the barrel of a rifle barely visible behind the single boulder amidst the Joshua trees and sagebrush. There wasn't supposed to be anyone out here except a woman with a trailer, and so far he'd seen neither. Drug dealers? Coyotes? His right hand itched to grasp his rifle from its scabbard attached to Lightyear's saddle.

He studied the area past the rock. Were there more? There was no other place to hide so completely. He didn't see anyone else. One delinquent he could handle. "Just out for a ride." He smiled crookedly. "Enjoying the day."

"Then turn around and enjoy the day somewhere else." The voice came again, but the rifle barrel remained steady. Whoever held that gun was in his element.

Shit. First he's tasked with doing Cole's dirty work, and then he has to come across some territorial drifter. He frowned at his remembered conversation with Cole.

"You want me to do what?" He tipped his cowboy hat up to stare at his cousin as if he'd just sprouted six legs and a long, poisonous tail.

Cole had the decency to look uncomfortable and lowered his leg from the rail of the training corral. "I don't have a choice. If she's been up there too long she could claim the land as hers under Arizona squatter laws. This Whisper woman needs to move her trailer off our land. You know the boundaries. She probably won't have to move very far. She's up over the rim of the north canyon."

Trace had little sympathy for the opposite sex at the moment, including his soon-to-be ex-wife, but he couldn't see kicking the woman off their land when she'd just saved Lacey's life. Didn't really speak of gratefulness to him. "Does Lacey agree with you?"

Cole started to turn. "It doesn't matter. It's what needs to be done."

Trace stepped in front of his cousin, not the least bit intimidated by Cole's scowl. "You can at least wait until after New Year's. Shit, with this kind of 'thank you,' you'll be lucky if the woman doesn't seek us out and kill us all in our beds."

"Just do it." His cousin stepped around him and strode toward the house.

There was no way this scenario was going to go well for Cole and possibly for the rest of them. To hear Lacey talk about Whisper, the woman walked on water, able to shoot a flower bud on a saguaro cactus from a half mile away.

Trace pulled off his hat and wiped the sweat from his forehead with his bandana then stuffed it back in his pocket and lowered his Stetson. He liked Lacey. She seemed to be a decent woman, one of the few left. She was going to be fit to be tied.

He grinned. Now that was something he'd like to see. It would serve Cole right for being so ungrateful and sending him to do the dirty work. Trace turned back toward the corral to find Lightyear, the mahogany-colored bay with black points that he liked to ride, standing near him. Ignoring the horse's face, he patted its withers. "I guess you and I are going to cause some trouble, boy."

The horse shook its head to dislodge a fly, but Trace chuckled. "No, not for us, but for your righteous owner." He entered the corral and carefully bridled Lightyear with a unique technique he'd developed. The horse was far too sensitive around his face, thanks to an encounter with a traveling swarm of bees.

Lightyear's face had swelled so much he could barely breathe. His owner had left him for dead, but a caring neighbor had called animal welfare. Cole and his vet had nursed the poor horse back to health over a year ago, but it still couldn't stand having its face touched.

Once Trace had the bridle in place, he added the saddle blanket, saddle and cinched the strap. Patting the horse on his side one more time, he mounted.

"Let's get this over with, buddy." Trace kicked Lightyear into a trot and they headed out to the canyon. His cousin had a big heart for horses, but when it came to people who didn't toe the line, he had no give at all.

Too bad Trace hadn't had the same strict rules for right and wrong as Cole had. Instead, he'd been blinded by a love that wasn't reciprocated and would soon lose everything he'd worked so hard for. He should have known. He would never get involved with a down-on-her-luck woman again.

In the meantime, he had a roof over his head and a job he enjoyed. Most of the time.

Now wasn't one of those times.

"Today would be nice. I got better things to do than shoot and bury trespassers. Turn your fancy ass around and get out of here." Though the voice definitely sounded irritated now, he smiled inside at the man's confidence.

Careful to keep his hands still, Trace cocked his head. "Then we have a problem. You see, this is my cousin's land and I'm not the one trespassing."

After a minute or two of no response, but with the rifle barrel still steady, Trace slowly moved his right hand down by his leg. The problem was, even if he did get to the rifle, he was a sitting duck up on Lightyear.

"Who's this supposed cousin?"

At the question, he stilled. Maybe he wasn't talking to a criminal. This could well be the husband of Lacey's Whisper. Preferring to settle the issue peaceably with no one getting hurt, most especially himself, he leaned forward in the saddle, hiding his right hand completely from view. "Cole Hatcher. His fiancée Lacey was up here recently."

"No, she wasn't."

Ah, the man knew who Lacey was. Trace listened intently as a muted swearing and grumbling came from behind the rock. He couldn't quite make out any particular words except "hell."

Grasping the rifle in his hand, he gave Lightyear a tap with his right foot. The horse started to move forward.

"I said turn around!"

Trace moved his left hand toward Lightyear's face. "Whoa, it's okay, buddy." He scratched beneath the horse's ear and Lightyear reared. Gripping the horse with his knees, he swung the rifle around and shot the rock where the barrel was visible.

"Dammit." The barrel moved then. "Freaking-a, what the hell are you doing? I could have shot you."

He still felt like a sitting duck, but since the man hadn't shot him yet, it meant he wasn't trigger-happy. "Show yourself."

A laugh sounded from behind the boulder. A very husky, feminine laugh and Trace's pulse accelerated.

"Now why would I do that?"

The voice was no different, but as Trace imagined a woman instead of a man, it no longer felt threatening. Instead, it had his imagination running wild without any clothes. Intrigued, his curiosity got the best of him. "Are you Whisper?"

The silence was deafening and he brought the rifle up again. He may have imagined that feminine tone. He hadn't been with a woman since he was served the papers for the divorce. He should probably find himself a one-night stand soon or he'd be thinking the fence post was a woman.

"Who wants to know?"

"I'm Trace, Cole's cousin. He sent me up here to talk to you."

Again silence. There was no way the rifle-bearer was a woman. Women weren't that patient, or that quiet, at least not in his experience.

A figure unfolded itself from behind the rock and Trace's breath stuck in his lungs. Startling silver eyes peered at him from beneath a worn, brown-leather cowboy hat. Beneath those eyes was a straight, elegant nose, high cheekbones and full lips that remained closed. A stubborn jaw anchored the lower face while small wisps of black hair framed the sides, the rest tied back somehow.

"So talk."

Trace blinked, letting the rifle go slack. As he took in the rest of the image, his interest cooled. The woman wore a loose red-and-black flannel shirt, a brown leather vest, a handgun stuffed into the waist of her baggy jeans and square-toed cowboy boots that had seen better days. Alarm bells went off in his head. A down-on-her-luck woman. Shit. "Are you Whisper?"

Her nod was barely discernable.

"Hello, miss. I understand you have a trailer up here."

Again, a slight nod.

He wasn't used to silent women. His wife talked nonstop, mostly about what she needed. Lacey, who he actually thought was a decent woman, also needed to fill in the silence as well, but at least with important stuff.

His task was important, at least to Cole. "Can I see it?"

"Why?"

So I can tell you it's on Hatcher-Williams land and you need to move it. He glanced down at the rifle held loosely in her hand. Lacey's comments on what a great shot Whisper was had him rethinking his plan. Maybe the straightforward approach wasn't the best. "Lacey said you lived up here with someone."

"Yeah, my uncle." She still didn't move, but her gaze flicked between him and Lightyear.

Interesting. "Can I talk to him?" Maybe a man-to-man conversation would be easier.

Her lips quirked up on one side just slightly, just enough to rivet his gaze. "Sure. This way."

Trace took a moment to get Lightyear moving, his mind still stuck on the image of her full, feminine lips, but once he set the horse to a walk in between the Joshua trees, it became apparent that riding wasn't the easiest way to move forward.

Quickly, he jumped down and carefully pulled the reins over Lightyear's head so they wouldn't brush along the horse's face. He grasped them low and guided the horse between trees, keeping the blue jeans and brown vest in sight.

Whisper's long, straight black ponytail swished back-and-forth with her stride, catching his attention and holding it to the point he almost walked into a prickly pear cactus. Shit, as if the Joshua trees didn't make this area of the high desert a challenge enough to navigate. No wonder he and his cousin had rarely ventured up here as kids. How the hell did they get a trailer in here?

Finally, they emerged into what looked like a natural clearing of hard-packed earth and there sat a large trailer covered in the dust of the environment. In front of it sat a single Adirondack chair and a chiminea. With a quick scan, he could see a shed to the left and slightly behind it, a cord running to the trailer. A generator? To the right of the home sat an ATV under the shade of a wooden carport-type structure.

"He's in there." Whisper grabbed his attention once again and he raised an eyebrow.

"You're not coming in?"

"It's too close in there with more than two people." She waved her hand toward the trailer even as she sat in the chair, the rifle on her lap. "Go ahead. You can introduce yourself."

Trace released Lightyear's reins. "Stay there, buddy. I'll be right back." Anxious to talk to a man instead of Lacey's odd friend, Trace strode quickly to the trailer and knocked.

"Oh, go ahead in. Uncle Joey won't bite."

Then why did he suddenly have the feeling she wasn't giving him the whole story.

Trace's Trouble (Last Chance Series: Book 2) (http://www.
lexipostbooks.com/traces-trouble/)

For updates, sneak peeks, and special prizes, sign up to receive
the latest news from Lexi at www.lexipostbooks.com.

ALSO BY LEXI POST

Contemporary Cowboy Erotic Romance

Cowboy's Never Fold (Poker Flat Series: Book 1)

When cowboy Wade Johnson honors a promise by working at a nudist resort, he discovers that to win the sexy owner's heart he must go all-in, which could mean baring more than his soul.

Cowboy's Match (Poker Flat Series: Book 2)

When cowboy firefighter Cole Hatcher is called to a fire at the Poker Flat Nudist Resort, he is sure his ex-girlfriend Lacey is to blame. But the more he investigates, the more the heat builds between them, and the more his gut tells him he's going to get burned.

Christmas with Angel (Last Chance Series: Book 1)

Cole Hatcher and Lacey Winters may not agree on where to spend Christmas day, but when Angel's abusive former owner decides to take matters into his own hands, the couple pulls together to focus on what's most important.

Trace's Trouble (Last Chance Series: Book 2)

Divorced cowboy, Trace Williams, must evict a squatter from his cousin's ranch. Unfortunately, he's not quite sure what to make of the feisty woman who understands animals better than humans. All he knows is she's a whole lot of trouble.

Logan's Luck: (Last Chance Series: Book 3)

Logan Williams has plenty of luck. The problem is, it's all bad.

Coming Soon

Paranormal Erotic Romance

Pleasures of Christmas Past (A Christmas Carol Series: Book 1)

Masque

Passion's Poison

Passion of Sleepy Hollow

Sci-fi Erotic Romance

Cruise into Eden (The Eden Series: Book 1)

Unexpected Eden (The Eden Series: Book 2)

Eden Discovered (The Eden Series: Book 3)

Coming 2016

ABOUT LEXI POST

Lexi Post is a New York Times and USA Today best-selling author of erotic romance inspired by the classics. She spent years in higher education taking and teaching courses about the classical literature she loved. From Edgar Allan Poe's short story "The Masque of the Red Death" to Tolstoy's *War and Peace*, she's read, studied, and taught wonderful classics.

But Lexi's first love is romance novels. In an effort to marry her two first loves, she started writing erotic romance inspired by the classics and found she loved it. Lexi believes there's no end to the romantic inspiration she can find in great literature. Her books are known for being "erotic romance with a whole lot of story."

Lexi is living her own happily ever after with her husband and her cat in Florida. She makes her own ice cream every weekend, loves bright colors, and is never seen without a hat.

www.lexipostbooks.com

Made in the USA
Middletown, DE
27 May 2018